GHOST TRAIN
NO EXITS

Ghost Train No Exits: CK Kuya's GTNE

MICHAEL A BLACKHALL

Contributions by Fareeha Khan

Ghost Train No Exits
Copyright © 2024 by Michael A Blackhall

Contributions by Fareeha Khan

Tellwell Talent
www.tellwell.ca

ISBN
978-0-2288-1752-9 (Hardcover)
978-0-2288-1753-6 (Paperback)
978-0-2288-1751-2 (eBook)

Table of Contents

Michael A. Blackhall
Toronto, M2R 1P1
14165095805
ck.kuya.project8020@gmail.com

GHOST TRAIN NO EXITS

CK KUYA – BOOK-1, GTNE VOLUME – 1

(2020-2040 QUEST)

CODE: GTNE-B1-V1-0001-CK KUYA PROJECT
8020-First-Introduction Volume.
Michael A. Blackhall (Author's: First of six future Fictional Novels)

TORONTO UBER-DRIVER STORY
COMING-SOON…

AFTER COMPLETED 35,000 TRIPS & 100,000 PASSENGERS,
DRIVER EXPERIENCE 2-NOVEL FROM 2026…

Michael A. Blackhall (Author's: 2-future novels…)

Michael A. Blackhall
Toronto, M2R 1P1
14165095805
ck.kuya.project8020@gmail.com

GHOST TRAIN NO EXITS BOOK-1

**The Introduction / General Contents / The
Sources / How it Began / Preface**

- Michael A. Blackhall (Author), Toronto, Ontario, Canada.
  - Fareeha Khan (Associate-Assistant, Developer
  & Co-author) Lahore, Pakistan.

**CK Kuya Project - GTNE Book-1 (From
2018 – 2020) [delay-2020-2024]**

A FICTIONAL STORY: (SUPERNATURAL, PARANORMAL AND
SPIRITUAL FROM GHOSTLY PERSPECTIVE).

- Written as a love story and romance by spirits in love.
  It's a drama, suspense and mild horror depiction.

GTNE-B1-V1, 1ST Volume: <u>THE INTRODUCTION</u>:

[The initial publication due in 2020 was pushed back to this point due to COVID-19 Pandemic.]

This first volume is now being presented as greater than a teaser starter, but as an introduction to the main characters.

This will be followed by the first normal read-length novel by 2025.

This book (GTNE-B2-V1a) has given way for the following developments of the company to be established:

- *For (Cultural Art & Entertainment business) The Jamaican Cultural Performing Arts.*
- *BAWT-CityTOURs, Affiliates: A Toronto Limousine Service, Tour Operator & Sightseeing business.*
- *The Company is currently being introduced at website <www.batravel.ca>. LINK: <bawt.ca>*
- Purchase direct Limo-rides at: <limo.bawt.ca>
- An organized strategy for hiring the homeless people globally where no other company or corporations will or would:

  o See the Web: https://batravel.ca/empowering-communities-worldwide/
  o Each member (person) associated with the corporation as one of the (homeless) individuals, will be associated via this link or similar <www.10-bawt.ca> or <10-bawt.com>.
  o Their job is to do exactly what they do daily for earning small change.
  o BAWT-Inc & CK Kuya is replacing the piece of cardboard paper that states as follows:
  o (1) Homeless: (2) Have hungry children, (3) Have no job, (4) Any small change helps.
  o Follow the above link to see how it works.

NOTE:

These are the CK KUYA plans. This is fictionally assumed to be as the fictional guardian angel. A ghost among us on the earth.

Ghosts are real entities! Follow your gut earnestly and you'll be convinced. Watch initially for the signs! They don't happen all at once!

- From my Gut to over 34,000 Rideshare Uber/Lyft Trips, Toronto to 100,000 Riders,
- From my Gut to learn some 30 language or cultural greeting phrases (Not fluently),
- From my Gut to full-time college student at age 67 to become certified TICO, Ontario, Travel advisor/ Agent/ Agency,
- From my Gut to being trained as Limousine driver/owner, A plan to develop to a five vehicle fleet of Limousine vehicles.
- From my Gut to this manuscript for up to a series of unknown number of books of which stories I already know about quite well,
- From my Gut to develop the entire website content where I had no knowledge or knew how. See [*website <www.batravel.ca>. LINK: <bawt.ca>*].
- From my Gut to formulate how to hire all homeless individual worldwide. They all can earning as highly trained individuals being a beggar,
- From my Gut to six phases and sub-phases with still the larger of the six phases still to be introduced in five to 30 years in future.
- From my Gut I was hired to go to Massachusetts, USA to the place JP where the CK Kuya stories begins. A total journey of nearly 1900KM.
- From my Gut to the most significant of all my findings and discoveries yet to be confirmed.

<u>**INTRODUCTION R&R**</u>: (Relative and Relatable)

This introduction serves to provide a source of <u>PREVIEW INTRODUCTION</u> to the readers and to help with pulling one through some of the sections that one will come upon, where there will be questions pending as this being a fictional meant for a supernatural and paranormal depiction.

On many of pages, the contents will be found to be relative, and relatable to most readers.

While in most cases, relatable to previous thoughts of things never understood before, and where one might have had those feelings that were constantly lingering; however never understood. This may now be received as a confirmation in some or most of those cases.

Making the Read (Hopefully) Interesting, Intuitive, & For Fun.

It provides insightful options on life, otherwise, the flipsides on how our realities may be viewed differently, that, should you set this book down, you will be left with a thirsty longing, and a desire of wanting for more when considering the opposite side from here. Many or most clairvoyant individuals will know what this all means to them.

So, is the author then clairvoyant? He never said! Things always just seems to fall in their given places.

The book and contents do have that power of just pulling you right back inside for more of its contents. It is that interesting, spiritually intuitive, mind boggling and even fascinating, though fictional it may be.

One will also be inspired by the consciousness of how things may be done better, but differently, with a much better approach.

As one proceeds with reading through the book, take notes of the contents, as there to be found many clues, and phrases within; for trivia games, and questions that follow this novel in some time.

- **(To Inspire - Not for Gambling)**
- This is original and meant for loads of fun with very significant prizes. Please note this is not for gambling.

- **(To Inspire Insightful Spiritual Significance)**
- The focus is first and foremost by the author's perspectives; to inspire an in-depth view; by the insights available within the contents, that; the People have SPKN (spoken). "**Stop People-K Now**!" In set for the Performing Arts, Triple Treat, Live Musical, Following Book-2 publication.

There is absolutely no need for killing! No benefits! It justifies nothing! It however alters one's spiritual progress. Because in all realms, dimension's, all sectors of life or otherwise, all space and time there are governance, having similar cause & effect repercussions, by the management of the various laws associated.

Cold blooded killing or otherwise has its punishments in all dimensions. But can any human able to kill a spirit? That, since humans are spirits hosts only and so the body dies in time but not the spirits that it is hosting.

The human (the body) is just the place where the spirit (we) lives for the duration that the human body is prolonged, till it becomes unrepairable. Does this mean that the occupants (Plural) also die? Plural yes! That because; no house was ever built for just one occupant. Even if that was the case and occupied by just one, that from time to time, that one does have visitors there.

- **(Participation Rewards Program** *{PRP}*)
- Readers are encouraged to register each copy of this and each published novel online,<ckkuya.com> where also the rewards games may be downloaded in some time; for Kool participation-prizes, which serve as part of our upcoming rewards program.

- **(JA-C-TOS)**
- Before writing the manuscript to this book, I had just completed a Travel & Tourism, TICO certification program, (i.e.: *Travel Industry Council Ontario, CAD*). I was in inclining for starting up <u>Jamaica Cultural Tour Operator Service</u> (*my main goal & charter*) when that idea was intercepted by CK Kuya forces and by spiritual persuasions. The most significant was for the fact as helpful to many nations of people.

THIS BOOK TITLE: *GHOST TRAIN NO EXITS*

From the numerous sources drawn from and for this <u>fictional</u> story, it is perceived and implied that; once the spirits of an individual human has exited from the deceased human body, which was the specific host for that or those specific spirits.

It (the spirit{s}) does continue to exist within a parallel zone, or universe somewhere (for lack of an exact or proper word, whether it being confirmable, or not).

Some refer to this parallel zone as being the "Spirit World," or "Purgatory," or "Limbo," and other names, depending on your culture. However; but no one has any perfect knowledge, tangible, or confirmable information as to exactly what happens, or takes place there, or whether truly exist or not, and it remains as an unknown; except by your personal faith.

In this <u>fictional</u> novel, the character refers to (on this side of life) as being "CK" or "Charli-Alice" and a full name being "Charli-Alice Kuya", along with the reference name being ayuЖuya, that is read on two plains being backward/forward because she returns from a parallel place referred above.

But while at the parallel side where she thinks she is on a train, she is identified as "Charli-K."

So; just like looking into a mirror, the reading is backward, hence the reason for the backward-forward Logo, ЖƆ and ayuK from her last name Kuya.

FYI: In speaking Jamaican patois; Kuya: means to look, inquire, observe, expression of surprise, wow! Explore, learn, absorb, or to; INTELEGATE YOURSELF!

However, a few months after I began writing, I learned that in another culture, "KUYA" means kinship, of another older male person, whereas; of that, I had no idea.

Had I thought about the kinship of my novel character, CK, I probably would have named her "my Ate" instead. It's a name used in the Philippines in reference to an older female person.

Also, as I write, I came to realized that CK was pregnant by about 7-months and should have delivered a male child by sometime early in 1950 and be about 1 year older than me. Hence my Kuya.

I also found it to be random, that in Toronto, North York, that I have driven mostly Filipinos and whereas of the near 400 of my riders out of 20,000 rides, that about 25 passengers who have requested my book are from the Philippines. Many are my Kuya and Ate, and many refers to me as "Brother." Then I would respond to them "Magandang: umaga, hapon, or Gabi."

RANDOM CONTEMPLATIONS

Having reviewed these things, & my thoughts, which after I have written them, realized that I never really gave any prior thoughts, before writing them.

According to my story, CK might very well have attached the spirit of her unborn son on me; when there was a devastating hurricane that hit Jamaica, and when I was still newborn in 1951, while she (by her spirit) was there helping a lot of people as by the Supernatural, and Angelic manifestation.

Putting 2 & 2 together, I feel that; she has been visiting me for all those years, perhaps because of her son's spirit in me. Hence my Kuya! Yea! Really CraZzzze thoughts I know! Hence fictional!

While all this may be, or could be very true, I have no perfect knowledge here, and it remains a fictional story. However, you the readers will be able to help me decide on what could be true or remaining as a fictional story. I invite you to put your 2 & 2 together as well, see what you come up with? Please do!

BEFORE CK'S DISAPPEARANCE

Before her disappearance and unconfirmed death, Bo; her fiancé had given a birthday gift to her on their first real date, which was a golden broach, made with her initials being "CK" which she wore perhaps every day.

After her assumed death, whenever she crosses over to this side of mortality, her broach now seen and reads as backward letters.

<u>Hilarious!</u>
It's too early in the story, so don't be sleeping off now! Stay up with me a while; will you?

A THOUGHT CONCERNING WHEN WE ARE IN LOVE

Has anyone ever seriously noticed and contemplate in dept; concerning some or many of the things that humans are capable and able to do, when we have genuinely fallen in love?

That of being inspired, when there was another (unseen) force that was at work with us, and with regarding the elements, and the bigger obstacles of nature against our thoughts, and feelings.

<u>SONG</u>: ["I Knew You Were Waiting for Me," by; Aretha Franklin]

Lyrics: When <u>the river</u> was deep, I didn't falter, When the <u>mountain</u> was high, I still believed, When <u>the valley</u> was low it didn't stop me.

<u>SONG</u>: ["No Scars to Your Beautiful," by; Alessia Cara]

"<u>We're stars</u> and we're beautiful"

<u>SONG</u>: ["<u>We Are</u>," by Toby Lightman]

We are <u>kings and queens</u> and <u>flying machines</u>…

We are <u>shiny jewels</u>… We are hope… <u>We are comets</u> flying through the air.

HOW IT ALL BEGAN

Having the feeling that I needed my daughter with me to be able to accomplish the task which has been given to me; I finally confronted her, only to be told the following.

"Dad; I am working in the legal professional field while you are trying to start up a business in travel and tourism; so I cannot work with you."

Other thoughts, intuitions, inspirations, dreams, random memories, certain abilities, and realizations came upon me, and I continued to pursue her assistance when finally she said this…

"Dad; you know what? What you are telling me sounds very interesting, so in order for me to understand what you are thinking to do, I want you to…"

Get this! The key which unlocked my Chest, containing all of my instructions, stories, realizations, contemplations, unknown-plans, dreams, random memories, thoughts which I contemplate for years, and years and didn't know what to do with them.

Even previous instructions which I received before so long ago and I did not know what to do with them, and to all that I am writing here in this GTNE novel now finally make sense to me.

From that above conversation, I also realized to the sixth phase of CK Kuya developments.

My daughter: She said, "Write a short story." "Something that I can read!" Once I agreed and said, "ok! I will write.» That was all that was needed. I wrote her a two-page short intro story with regards to my C-TOS (Cultural travel Tour Operator Service) idea for Jamaica, exclusive of this CK story, which became part of the last pages of this novel story. ***This is how and where it began.***

WHO DO I THANK TO THIS POINT

The list is too long, which includes one of my editors (Sahar) for coaching expertise.

Naomi-Joy Blackhall

I am very grateful to my daughter, who is/was unaware of this writing, and, of her part with the development of this story and novel that took me only five months to write it.

I am happy that; from knowing and believing what I do now, I am also happy that I have participated in procreation and have done all my part in the fathering, parenting, and raising up of three children to adulthood, and whom I do love. I am very grateful to have done my part throughout their growing up. And that's just it. All should and must do your part. Perform in all that you are called or assigned to do, for when it's done it's done!

<u>Marina, Margarita, and Jose</u>

Much gratitude to those of my acquaintances for their amazing support. Their encouragements of getting out and include some physical exercises, where time does not allow me. And then to mind the things that I eat and so much more; too many to mention here.

Cliff, Peter, Howie

This is my favorite garage, mechanics, and managers at 2805 Dufferin Street, at AGR. Here, I received the most in car-care. Very prompt, courteous, respectful, and very detailed in service. Because of their excellent service and professionalism that I felt it important to mention in my book, which is by far the highest compliment that anyone could give to a community garage, and its associates.

To My Uber Riders

That within a year, there has been some 400 of my riders who have encouraged, and have also inspired me to continue writing whereas over 300 have sent their emails saying that; "I can't wait to read your book!"

Some have even given me a few subtitles for my book; simply because of their interest and communication towards my writing.

I am grateful to have been a Toronto Uber driver, whereas I have learned further how to provide the excellent customer service, to have maintained a (4.91-4.97) of their 5★★★★★ rating, and to also accomplish and maintained as an Uber Top Diamond Driver.

And yes! Deep down I am also grateful to the Uber company, for approving me as a driver to their platform of "Ridesharing concept" as a driver.

Because of that opportunity, I was able to connect with up to over 100,000 individually riders from the year 2014 to current year 2024, whereas at some point after publishing the series of CK Kuya books, I will most definitely be writing another, to tell my stories from my ridesharing experience, because many riders have inquired, and have suggested.

Fareeha Khan. [☆☆☆☆☆] Whois:

- A Trusted Business Associate,
- Motivator, Online-Website Remote Assistant,
- Most Dedicated Go-To Person since the last four years,
- Manuscript-reviewer, Commentor, Summary provider.
- LAST TO MENTIONED CERTAINLY NOT THE LEAST!

In this listing, each item speak for the excellent service provided by Fareeha throughout the last 4-years of hard work in building the business to this point of writing, rewriting, edits after edits due to COVID-19 Pandemic.

GIVING BACK:
My largest group of supporters were my ridesharing rider customers. So, for in line of giving back, by an email (bawt@batracel.ca) or WhatsApp +1(416-509-5805, each and (other than all minors) **"EVERYONE-CAN" (Pmc)** now request a Complementary Luxury Vacation Accommodation Gift to vacation destinations globally. NO PURCHASE NECESSARY! TAX & HOTEL FEES may be applicable.
NOTE: Per met criteria and of age (Pmc).

'CULTURAL ART & MENTO THROWBACK'
This development & project was conceptualized in Toronto, Ontario, Canada as presented by Michael A. Blackhall.

<u>NOTE: In respect to privacy policy</u>

This first novel (GTNE-B1-V1-1ST-Volume), Following (GTNE-B2-V1a-Volume), (GTNE-B3-V2), and (GAQ-B4-V3), (Uber-Driver-Rider-A-fare-B5-V4) nor any other novels following were not and will not be meant as an attempt to convince, nor preach to anyone per our published contents.

None of the books in the CK Kuya series represent any one religion, culture, language, gender, personal orientation to life choices, or nation of people, people color, or others. Absolutely no discrimination meant and hoping none taken as such.

These stories are really from random inspirations, as well as ideas that came along fictionally.

While much of the contents are true to life or not, others were inspired by many true events and spiritual derivatives however they were percieved.

Spiritual, because I, the author, from my gut-feelings, I believe whole heartedly that we; (all humans) are all spirits and separate from the human body which is the host for us being spirits, that also gives the spirit abilities for accomplishing physical things, provide the motives for the spirit to gain necessary and required experiences.

Thus, we see and acknowledge that just one of our lifetimes is vastly insufficient, hence it is stated that; "You must be born again! And by the very practicum suggested that; to be born is by the very means provided for giving birth or rebirth, even per the example of the documented immaculate Conception.

That should one thinks or feels that God will make up the difference for what we did not accomplish or learn, then we must rethink! For all the Prophets of old or current had to accomplish their various assignments on their own for God has no need for making up any differences we lack.

For whatever we perceive God to be, the plan for us all is for learning and to learn by all the various and multiple means, tools, elements, channels and from every opportunity given us in life where there are no short-cuts, because we have eternity to live it over till, we learn it.

Or if by some chance we; by the gift of free will and choice we have refused to learn or by will that we'd done things from which are unforgiving. Then that's our choice that no one of us allowed to judge on those things by Ameen and Ameen! or Amen & Amen!

For the rest, I personally don't exactly know for certain, or exactly from what source all were derived, except by my very strong and persuasive gut-feelings, which are, and remain spiritual.

It is however true, that I cannot and will not say that I've had any visitation or representative stating from any burning bush that remains green and unsinged.

Since each person was born with the gift of understanding, and a sense of detecting by your spirit when some things are not true, it is recommended that one must resort to those of your inherent senses, knowledge feelings and judge to understand if any of these things means well to oneself or others?

Therefore, I simply continued with the writing as it all flows out, as though being dictated page after page unto: The End of this series.

- **<u>HENCE THIS REMAINS FICTIONAL:</u>**
  I implore you: "Stay with me some more! Will you? It gets way better from here!" But pull-up your pants, lace up your shoes, keep your eyes peeled, and hold on tightly to your seats.

The various parts, chapters or in the following books:
- May be found to be quite hilarious, spooky, it's gut-pinching, emotional,
- It may as well be referred to as very jaw dropping like; "I had no idea!"
- Otherwise; "This makes perfect sense now!"
- "I never look at things this way before!"
- It's fascinating! It is also absolutely what the world needs now!

Over four hundred of my Uber passengers under two years has said, "OMG! I can't wait to read your book!"

- **People of multi-ethnicity:**

Those are people from every continent, every major country, and cultures of the world, ranging from nine years young (one) with both parents present, to eighty-five years of age.

I have had people told me; I have been <u>an atheist,</u> but now I'll have to think twice!

CODE: GTNE-B1-V1-0001-CK KUYA PROJECT 8020-FIRST EDITION-INTRO.

- **SPECIAL NOTES ON CHAPTERS:**

Since this first novel was published as a <u>first volume for the purpose of an introduction,</u> in that it was due from 2019 prior COVID-19 pandemic, so the chapters being used are the actual chapters of the full and original book manuscript. Only the selected chapters are being used in this edition volume-1.

Where contents have been added those will show as a chapter # - # or such as: (Chapter 29-1). Even so, in the full version (book-2) there will be added or original information missing from the first edition, for providing the full content and meaning once the live performing arts musical production from this GTNE novel series begins.

CHAPTER – 11 ЖС

THE FINDING OF ONE'S LOVE
<u>**SONG:**</u> **[For All We Know, by; Andy Williams]**

He thought he'd first laid eyes on her (CK) someplace in Saint Paul, Minnesota, but unclear with only a vague memory of her.

There was no contact, or exchange of words.

She would have been less than fifteen years old, but there was something about her that tells him that he has seen her before somewhere.

She was shy yet bright, and when he looks at her, she would be seen as to glow brightly and seems to wear a brilliant halo encapsulating her entire body.

Her demeanor caused his eyes to be fixed on her as though standing frozen.

The attraction sets him in a transfixed attentiveness, and fully drawn to her, almost as though she possessed him from the first day they spoke.

There was no way to resist her attraction that compelled his profound and intrinsic gaze.

Bonding never requires any attempt or was ever necessary, it was as though they were naturally meant for each other or so it seems.

Perhaps it's for some other special; and or heavenly meaning to this attraction that no one else will ever discover.

It was as though they grew up together since she was under sixteen and they fell in love at that early age. They couldn't imagine that anything other than their love could have a place between them.

(A different Kind of Love)
In a park as teenagers, they carved their initials and frequently carve love stories, love letters deep in the bark of young trees.

Prior to falling in love with CK, Bo (as she named him), had already found a different kind of love in his life, one that held the same effects as any young motorcyclist racing on down a city highway.

<u>SONG</u>: [The Orange Blossom Special, by; Johnny Cash]

That; due to an obsession; one of those other passions, that most young convertible sports car drivers possess; along with heavy adrenalin rush; would be cause enough to display as peacocks do.

That also; while the summer wind would be allowed to comb through their hair with shirttails dancing in the wind behind them while as they race on down the boulevard; well over the posted city highway speed limits.

And thus, with the loud rumble of their exhausts, and race engines they were empowered.

That; and the love and passion of this young man so early in his life, would be to ride on freight trains to wherever it was going.

The sound of the steam engines would be like a lullaby. To him, that could easily be described as a tonic for relaxation, that could put a person to a sleep mode in no time.

Anyone musically inclined could play a melody by it, and then add lyrics to make up a song as most have already done.

Boise J, or Bo had already begun to write songs as he learns how to play the guitar.

He would write, and write, yet not any of his good writings ever made it to public hands for recording or other possibilities that could have easily led to success.

With its gentle rocking and the black smoke-spitting up from its exhaust, was fascinating to him, and in so much that he was able to just be lost in the wind, on the rails, and be gone was he for several days, just looking around from city to city and then back again.

He would already be dreaming as soon as the train enters the pitch blackness of each tunnel, <u>WONDERING</u>! What scary experience he could find beneath each mountain he was passing through.

Being able to go through a mountain instead of over or around it, by that only, was already grandiose of an idea for him.

Many boys; since the first full-scale and working railway system; the steam locomotive was invented and placed in operation to public service found passion.

Many people became fascinated with trains, and some even became financially rich, from copying and making rhythm and blues from the various musical sounds of locomotive trains.

<u>Song</u>: The Wabash Cannonball, by; Johnny Cash

Since the language of music was already a part of Bo's early years and his inner disposition, he was able to hear and identify the various sounds of locomotives in a very natural, symphonic, and even orchestral way.

His abilities were such that; he was also able to identify various, and sequential genres of music to his ears which was a great talent for him.

(First Locomotive System - Bo's First Love)

It is public knowledge that the first working railway steam locomotive was built in the UK. In 1804 by Richard Trevithick, a British engineer born in Cornwall. This used high-pressure steam to drive the engine (steam engine).

As the train gets closer, it makes a rumbling sound.

As it leaves the station, it makes a steadily increasing chugging sound, especially when moving, gradually picking up speed, and in the distant against the cold nights of wailing winds.

The whistle can make the sound to be as pitiful and forlorn, which may also be described as despairing, mournful and a woe-be-gone noise.

A noise which may be used to spawn the eerie, ghostly, spine-chilling and hair-raising scare to a person, in as much as to imply fright of something supernatural, that sounds almost as from something unearthly, mysterious, and unnatural, especially in a very frightening way.

Even when the train is coming to a stop the braking sounds make hisses, and screech as the train slows down till it stops.

All of which meant a great deal to Bo, and the reasons why he is so much fascinated by trains, and the only thing that could come close to measuring up with his CK. But now, in their secret lover's park, he now spent his lonely days, broken-hearted, and dreams forever that someday she'll return.

And so; for well over thirty years, the person he was so in love with, has gradually drifted from him, and from what he had hoped to accomplish with her by his side.

The Lord knows that he's been through a lot when considering that he was the last person to speak with Charli-Alice, and the last to see her alive. How many questions must he answer, do you think?

The fellows who had sung happy birthday to CK on her sixteenth birthday at that park, now grieves with Bo, with hopefully helping him get over, or find his girl who was his main squeeze and squeezed they did! With much laughter, with joy, gladness and radiant spirit of oneness and forever connected.

"But see!" Bo, look yonder! Said James (who was one of Bo's musician friends).

"I <u>WONDER</u>! What's the reason for those Police officers coming this way. More questions, do you think Bo?" "Oh God no! Not again."

Said Bo. Exclaiming harshly with some cuss words.

CHAPTER – 12 ЖƆ

WHAT ON EARTH COULD HAVE GONE WRONG?

SONG: [by Blue October. Title: Hate me]

The year is 1949. She is running, running, running as though, no place in particular, where she had to go, or that she was chasing after her man; thinking that he might have left on one of those freight trains he is used to going away on.

It was a time during or just after puberty, and he really trying to explore life's options not really understanding all that is involved when two people are committed to loving.

In some cases, lack of those experiences to forge sincerity does cause some folks to drift and enter avenues unapproved by the one you first fell in love with.

Entering uncharted, unplanned territories can and does return the effects of heartbreak, and confusion, which at times cause the wild and random confused decisions.

He's screaming and yelling in words-fight send her running to the valley of tears not knowing how to quench the flame of anger, and perhaps jealousy; that raged in his heart.

So, with fear and confusion, she ran, and ran, with no destination in mind she entered the open doors of the subway train and went for a long lonesome ride; unaware that that action would have led to a non-return trip.

CHAPTER – 13 ЖꙄ

WELL DID SHE EVER RETURN:

About the time, earlier in 1949, a stated name of Charlie had only one dime; as was the fare to get on and ride the city train, but since the city of Boston levied and penalized the citizens, the only way to get out of that levy was the hope, and if the mayoral candidate Walter A. O'Brien had won the mayoral election.

(A must-read! I invite you search it online.)

Then he; as promised, would have removed the levy which demands the riders to pay a fare of fifty percent at the destination, or before one was able to exit from each train ride.

When you read the various stories on Google, it seemed to me that a lot of people were benefited while Walter O, was the only one that was politically concerned about Charlie, and others, but since he lost the election in an embarrassing fashion, was basically blacklisted and ran out of town, from the stories we read regarding.

Unfortunately, no one talks anymore about Charlie, who was never heard from, or about.

The conversations, stories and speculations are only regarding the sides, and rationales of the MTA company (Metropolitan Transportation Authority, and the various political agendas.

No one brings up the matter for those, and all the Charlies who were never allowed to exit the train, or able to identify those who may have died in the various train wreckage of 1949-50, or thereabout, and who never had an Itinerary in those times.

SONG: [Charlie on The MTA; by; The Kingston Trio]

NOTE:

Well, the story has been written and told and whether true or false, I inclined to believe to the most parts, and assume that; this story was true; otherwise mostly true.

"But true or false me no mek no call, an yu tek et de waay yu want et!" Jamaican talk: MEANING:

But true or false, I declare as fictional by gut-feelings, you may accept this story the way that you feel or want to. That is, your choice, as the story is relative and relatable.

CORELATE: *Observe the names of places. Why are they the same?*

The train to "Kendall" square train-station, (USA), Jamaica Plains, that Charlie rode on to get home: (Crashed somewhere 1949 -1950), Killed, but CK's, body was never identified.

VS.
The train to "Kendal" train-station, (Caribbean), Jamaica, W.I. (Crashed near the "Kendal" station Sept. 01-1957). Killed 200, CK (Angel?) rescued many people before help arrived.

Much of the information is found on the website for mbta.com/history, other sites as having been published up to February 1951. Website: digifind-it.com/oghs/data/ogt/1951/1951-02-09.pdf.

CHAPTER – 14 ӜƆ

MAYORAL ELECTION 1949

Unfortunately, Walter A. O'Brien, (candidate) he never won that Mayoral election in Massachusetts, USA.

Charli-Alice had not realized, concerning the train fare levy, that was in effect at that time, or perhaps she was too angry when she got on the train and didn't think about securing the exit fare change, and so, she could not exit the train, which should have been bound through Kendall square station MA, USA.

But further on you will need to help the writer with or regarding "The Mystery About CK Kuya," and a train that crashed in; or near the <u>Kendal station in Jamaica, W.I., in</u> the Caribbean on September 01, 1957, <u>*"Killing"*</u> nearly, or above 200 people to include those died after the fact and due to the crash at Kendal.

(Perhaps in one of the following volumes)

That story regarding the Jamaica (Caribbean) Kendal station crash was written and for unknown reasons, some mysterious persons were mentioned in that book entitled the *"Reaper of Souls"* the author; Beverly East, which connection has been made herein. I feel it is no coincidence whatsoever.

Other ghostly matters have been mentioned in that book along with other many tales you can hear from the people of that region, however; they had no idea regarding what was really happening that involves "CK" until now.

What was written till now in certain literatures', books or documents etc., was from the human perspectives and based on what the human eyes, ears and voices were able to perceive, imply, denote or conjured for a story.

Nonetheless. All were limited to the human bare abilities and perhaps having no thoughts of any conjunctive interjections that could tie in between human connotation and the spiritual realm that humans can scarcely acknowledge, unless by some rare and random inspiration, otherwise by some means of clairvoyance receptors.

Things that were perceived as being ghostly, has only remained as ghostly, paranormal, or guise, concealing true nature until it has been figured out, i.e.: If ever!

He who was later realized to be she instead, may ride trains forever beneath the streets of Boston or wherever, thus he was named <u>"The man that never return."</u> Well did he ever return? No, he never returned, and his faith is still unlearned.

Even so much more now, that he is really, she as we now have this figured out, although the facts regarding gender are still very cloudy, and questionable when it comes to the spirits of humans.

That also; because we feel that there were more people who had perished, who were not able to exit the trains of Boston's MTA.

The fact regarding the exit fare may have affected more persons across the United States than Charli-Alice, and with the various fatal train crashes, it may also affect more people than we know.

It is the assumption now, that, for all those other persons, males or females who have been involved in train crash fatalities, who were never identified must be referred to as one of the Charlies.

SONG: [Speaking in Jamaican dialect]

So! Mi sey it agen "did dae eva return? No dae neva return, and dere fate is still anlear."

Now sadly forgotten, except for Charli-Alice Kuya (Charli K).

We became aware of Charli-Alice due to some random occurrences over the years, but the rest of the people who could never exit the MTA are unknown at this point in the story. We may yet locate others, or their spirits may find this author as CK did to have communicated this novel information and her various stories.

And we believe that due to Charli-Alice great love for Bo J, she persisted in trying to go home and to find Bo J. and leaving random clues for us in songs, and books and other random stories, dreams and jesters since we now pick up on a few of them that got this story started and rolling.

Many of the lyrics of various songs and stories help us to tell the story of Charli-Alice Kuya. More on that coming up!

Note dis:

Mi seh! "Tru ar false mi no mek no call, an a yu hav fe figa et out fe yu self, an bout wa yu com up wid."

WHERE I WENT WRONG:

Time and days went by Charli-Alice did not return home, and her Bo, received no letter, no Telegraph, no wire. Can you imagine how the parents and family are dealing with this listing as "missing person?"

<u>SONG:</u> [That's Where I Went Wrong, by; The Poppy Family]

Now, she; being sad and cries, and cries, and cries on the selfish reason why she ran and got on a train just so that she might just take the opportunity of contemplating on the reason that he, her one and only true love would choose to accuse her of things she had never done.

Then he wanting to leave town, to hop on freight trains, as was his passion, and to take off onto distant train tracks to leave her behind.

Charli-Alice never realized that the new law was in effect in the State of Massachusetts that each passenger must pay an exit-fare in the amount of 50% of the boarding fare which she did not have and thereby will never be able to get off the MTA train.

"Well; did she ever return? No; she never returns never got off, and her fate is still unlearned. She may ride forever on those lonely tracks of Boston, and, or wherever but she is known to never return.

<u>SONG:</u> [Charlie on the MTA, by the Kingston Trio]

O'Brien finished last in the mayoral race in the election of November 8, 1949.

By the mid-1950s, the strong leftist policies of the Progressives combined with the Red Scare, led to their public perception as communists (though they had no connection to the existing Communist Party). As a result, O'Brien disappeared into a political obscurity.

<u>THE MTA SMART CHARLIE-CARD DEVELOPMENT</u>

Today a smart card for Boston transit is called a "Charlie Card" as well as all those who are assumed lost between the rails; are now known to be a "Charlie-?" as in Charli-Alice being "Charlie-K" or just CK.

CHAPTER – 15 ЖƆ

A MAN IN DISPAIR (The year 1955-65)

He walked around, and around, and around the park, and when tired he would sit for hours as he pulls out his deck of cards and he plays the game of solitaire until it becomes too dark and lonelier before he goes to wherever place and lays down until he falls into peaceful shady summertime sleep.

SONG: [Solitaire; by; Andy Williams]

His only companion was his old dog "Mange", faithful and true since he wakes up every morning and his dog manage would be watching over him, hungry and scrawny as could be, but would always be by his side.

At morning light with mange, he travels in search of his Charli-Alice. Charli's one and only Love realized that he accused her badly that drove her on the run, now he walks the street and local places asking everyone if they have seen his lost love.

He began to write on some cardboard boxes and posting the notes everywhere with the hope that someone may have seen his Charli-Alice and give him a lead on where to look next.

SONG: [Have You Seen Her, by; Bill Anderson]

By this time 1955 Bo-J having travelled to so many various cities and towns asking and looking for leads of which has all lead him to no avail.

Bo-J vowed to never give up nor fosters the slightest intention of quitting his search.

Never giving in from his search and each day that comes along his love grows stronger and stronger, and that is what fuels his desire of finding his lost love.

SONG: [That's How Strong My Love Is, by; OV Wright]

Whatever the storm or weather system; he would suffer before quitting his search.

It's winter and through the frosty blizzard wind, and cold, cold Kentucky rains he forever drinks strong drinks to hopefully keeping him warm as he sleeps hungry and cold without any warm places to lay his head or rest his tired feet.

SONG: [Cold Kentucky Rain, by Eddy Rabbitt]

For drinks and tips and in his drunken state he would do a silly drunken dance that sometimes buys him a meal.

SONG: [Mister Bo Jangles; by; Eddie Rabbit]

Bo-Jangles learned to play the guitar at an early age, and although he never became a star, in his despair and desperation to survive he manage to get his hands on an old guitar and sings here and there for a few pennies' nickels and dimes in his old sweat-soaked and sweat-stained hat and from his singing.

SONG: [Bright Lights and Country Music; by; Bill Anderson]

When one town gave him no hints or promises he would hop on the next train, and he would ride and go off to the next town or state to restore his life-long search for his CK or Charli-Alice.

He had always had a passion for hitching rides on freight trains, but now he has a more urgent and valid reason for doing so.

SONG: [I get the fever, by; Bill Anderson]

There was this one time when his gut was telling something, but he could not figure out what it was that he was feeling.

Given the time of day and the route he was on, it could have been about the time when the train on which Charli-Alice rode, and this time the train was making its rerun, so they both have been on that very same train at the same time.

SONG: [The Tips of My Fingers, by; Conway Twitty]

Love sensation had brought those tingling feelings; to which; Bo-J had no ideas about what that was, and CK had not yet realized how to see what she wants to see; so, Bo was not visible to her either. In fact, CK not able to sense not by any spiritual sensory as the humans are created to perform for that is what the living human being offers the spirit it is hosting.

Well consider the humans as the spirit and our cars, trucks, or buses whatever we drive or fly. When we are not in the car, we do not have access to any of the components and gadgets until we have returned to the bridge, captain's chair or the driver's seat.

SONG: [Before I'll Set Her Free; by; Conway Twitty]

Bo-J had been thrown in jail for some disturbance which he caused and eventually went before the judge on trial to whom he pleads his case and his plight for finding his lost love.

Heaven knows, he's been in and out of courts and jail houses a bunch of times, because of this situation and this has been extremely hard on him, and for him to bear.

<u>SONG</u>: [The Winner, by Bobby Bare]

At other times Bo would get into Bar-fights which would ultimately land him in jail yet again for starting fights, as his emotions were always at an edge and hard to contain himself or his composure.

CHAPTER – 16 Жꓛ

ONLY YOU MAKE ME CRY:

It's been quite some earthly time passing by now, and Charli-Alice being on this train that she hopped on, have cried a river of tears why her man Bo-J, has so harshly accused her, and then he wanted to leave her behind, now she became desperate.

She needs to exit the train but is not allowed until she pays the exit fare of which she has no money which gives her another reason for crying "Another River of Tears."

She seeks desperately, complained seemingly, and vigorously, attempted somewhat with violent and aggression without avail she is still barred, disallowed exit without proof of payment for the exit.

<u>SONG</u>: [You're the Only One Can Make Me Cry, by; Concrete Blonde]

She cries and cries, and cries, buried in despair, buried in sadness, what else can she try, she needs to go home, she searched her thoughts, combed her intellect, devised plans without success.

She finds the staff's closet, "oh!" she thought in her mind, "uniforms ha!" no one is watching, she makes the change; pretending to be a conductor/porter of the train, but apparently that didn't work out, Charli-Alice realized that she's not able to exit the train.

It's been some time, some months that seems a very long time, and with each attempt to exit, Charli-Alice finds herself back in her coach, the only door way that she can go through are those of her sleeping bunk or any inside doors of the train; and she couldn't understand why.

Charli's Next plan is to befriend a passenger who she feels might be attracted to her with the hope that someone could help her for exiting this mysterious train that held her bound.

At some points, the vale between our reality and the parallel zone seems to become thin, and CK can connect with someone that she sensed able to see her and believing to be talking with her, although this may have been seduced by her influence, which was really an illusion.

CK can tap into their minds and understands what they're thinking about and find their desires of things they're mostly desiring, and then tries to fill their needs, be it whatever they're dreaming about, or hoping for which also fades away, but; however, leaving a memory they never forget. CK, however, does not seem to remember those incidents.

So far Charli-Alice has journeyed to every city wherever the train has travelled round, and round, and round, and so with every attempt for an exit, failed.

Each attempt of befriending a passenger, when it gets time to go, she realized she cannot exit the train, and found herself again in her coach and the cycle starts all over, thus; she forgets each last attempt made. Each one is like the first.

She cries, she cries, what can I do, I want to go home, I want to go and find Bo and mother.

<u>SONG</u>: [These Dreams; by; Heart the Band]

What Charli-Alice has not realized, was that; there had been a fatal train derailment 1949-50 somewhere, and many have died in that train wreck, but for CK this never happened, and she continues the search for a home.

It is regarded that when there is a sudden and frightful occurrence, and death takes someone, the spirit; due to the fright of it all, prematurely exits the body and not able to return because it does not realize what had happened.

Perhaps if realized, may have returned to the body at once if the body has not died. There is another observation, and it seems to be that when a ghost has exited from the body, in general the ghost does not look backwards. Hence having left the body forward, means the ghost cannot or never again sees its previously hosted body.

The train crashes of 1949-50 took many lives, and in reality; Charli's human-host life was snatched away from her, but still, Charli does not know this and still searches for her exit and her Bo. So; needing to go home she cries, and cries, and cries.

Where do I get off? I'm lost! I need to find a home repeating herself yet again.

The account of the various wreckages could be on one that Charli-Alice might have been on since we don't have the full details, and Charli-Alice had no official itinerary.

CHAPTER – 17 Ӝꙅ

WHAT MAY HAVE HAPPENED TO CK

This account was the closest we found that may imply where CK had been and where her train might have crashed.

There are many such stories available and as well as many varied information, however nothing to confirm. At least not to this point.

April 24, 1949 – United States – Smith County, Tennessee, Gordonsville, 10 persons were killed (or was it 9+1 other unidentified person perhaps Charli-Alice?) coming home from church at approximately 10:30 pm (Seems familiar for Jamaica crash), when a loaded locomotive hit them at a high rate of speed. The family, in two trucks, was <u>returning from a church service</u>.

It is certainly not the easiest to judge, to claim, to suggest, account for time, or justify exactly what happens between life and death.

The accident was reported sometime in 1949, that proclaimed, "Ten Killed When Train Strikes Truck; County's Worst Tragedy."

Many local senior citizens cling to grim remembrances of the terrible wreck that took place at 9:35 that Sunday night when a pick-up truck was smashed by a freight train a half mile east of Carthage Junction at the Gordonsville-Lancaster Road crossing about two miles east of Gordonsville.

For each of the following wreckages and many deaths, does open spirit-shifting portals and conduits for transporting the loose spirits across. Charli-Alice might have been hopping thru the various portals from the other side trying to get home.

I must however clarify that for every dimension there'll always be found law enforcement. This does happen right down to our human blood plasma circuitry system between the white & red blood cells as well among others that helps to keep humans and animals healthy.

However, while we are still investigating about Charli-Alice Kuya, the above hints do seem to be off for a few or number of reasons, that this is not the train that she was truly riding in,

CHAPTER – 18 ЖꙄ

MISTER BO JANGLES

By this time Bo J. has been throughout, from the north to the South searching for his beloved Charli-Alice, nowhere to be found. Bo has been in every Gin-joint and nearly every city, and in despair he drinks, and at some point, he would dance for tips and drinks since he does not always have funds available to him.

Most times that are spared after searching, he spent it in Gin-joints, and oft-times in County Jails because he drinks a bit, what else, but out of desperation and he blames himself for accusing his one and only.

Thus, he questions himself: "What can I do? Where can I go?" He contemplates as he reflects on the lyrics of a certain song, only to realize that he was going through the very similar situation as he compared himself with the lyrics of that song.

"I am Boise Jangles, and this bottle is supposed to be my best friend, the only one I can turn to, and lately, I've been turning every day, but the wine doesn't take effect as it used to, nor does it soothe my pains for losing my CK."

<u>SONG</u>: [Tonight; The Bottle Let Me Down; by; Merle Haggard]

CHAPTER – 19 ЖꝚ

MYSTERIES OF THE CHARLI-K GHOST

It is also believed that Charli-Alice had no travel clothing, so she used what was available, which was conductor, or porter uniforms.

There have been sightings at various moments in time of a mysterious female person form, which happened mostly at fatal disaster sites. Various trains, in various places, as well as other moments in time, sightings of mysterious ghost trains have been reported, and even the train prior to, and after the train of Nar, the mysterious ghost train.

Especially where people and first aid units have the opportunity of being arrived on site within minutes has been one of mysterious. In that, ofttimes it seems that people have been helped or assisted, and no one has any idea of how or what helped those people, nor does the people who have been helped had any clues or ideas except to say; ***"An angel or some spirits may have helped me."***

It became apparent that at these various sightings and places was the same female form, partly because she wore the very same unique backward golden CK-shape broach clipped against her right breast with the backward letters ЖꝚ (C & K).

With each sighting, this golden broach has appeared as letters written backward which suggest that she came from the other side or parallel zone or world.

REPEAT: Charli-Alice has been trying to get off that train where she and others have been bound for eternity. With each attempt, it seems to coincide with some unfortunate train fatalities after the fact, which suggests that she has no influences that would cause the crash to occur, but that of actional response to a portal, or portals and conduits being open to her.

Charli-Alice must have figured it out, and how to cross-over through these portals at times of a disaster, because she, or they have been cited at other random places.

When I have studied further, it seems as though; those portals have been deliberately placed where CK have been; as an invitation for to observe what she would do, having seen an opening, a way out.

Those portals also remind me that; God, having counselled Adam and Eve in the garden of Eden, have afterwards left the way to the garden unhidden, unguarded knowing that the spirit of Satan would find it and would enter in.

Moreover, CK; having jumped through and found people in dire straits, with choices faced with, what decisions would she make?

It is seen that, at each time that she has jumped and found people in need, she hesitated not, but to get to work and help as many as possible and be saving lives.

It was also seen that others have done the same jump as CK, and whereas, they became perverted in their doings.

In this writing, stating that many would fall to the dark side, doing the evil deeds and serving those who were involved with sorceries, and evil magic, and ghostly horrifying deeds and even to the wild sexual encounters mention or hinted herein, as well as may be found mentioned in the book ***"Reaper of souls"*** by, Beverly East. However, not completely wrong.

Perhaps the main reasons for this human life and living are for us our spirits to learn the higher knowledge offered because of the human interactions, and so when the human body dies it seems the only two things that follows that spirit from this life to the side of spirits is what the spirits learned and if married to the one and only soulmate of that spirit for there can only be just one but not anyone. Eve (Hawa) was the specific female and there could not be any other or modified otherwise.

No one can return to God or from where the spirit originates unless it was perfectly balanced and complete, even as Adam was; when at first created, having his female side returns to him or him to her in marriage while connected to their human hosts.

Note that the ties that binds the two is the same felt that confirms soulmates that cannot be confused. It is by far acknowledged that people in marriage when with their soulmates are usually for life and no other else that follows when one has died.

Even their lack of knowledge of their SM does not allow them to any other partner for the rest of their lives. While Bo had no knowledge of such as maybe reality, yet from early 20s when CK want missing could never bring himself to anyone else even as his friend Sally had tried for many years and still he could not give himself to her or any other.

Although not knowing, there is that bond that remains with the individuals once the soulmate was found. The bond to the most part is made once the mates have been found, whether married or not and once, they have touched skin to skin, even by the simple handshake. Nothing but human death alone can separate them for life having touched each other skin.

Similarly, if they are in constant communications can sense each other in multiple ways as though they were twins. They draw pains and pleasures even in distance lands and while not knowing are able to find their mates while on vacation in other lands.

There is that certain inherent and similar, even familiar aura that draws the mates by the various communications and verifications' felt and confirms. The mates can readily sense that there is no other for them, enough to overpower their emotions and sexual desires.

It would also appear that Charli-Alice may have been switching forms for every attempt of getting off the train, also that she and others may not have had any choice as to what country or city she/they appear, or whether on a ship, train or plane, or other, but at every turn she finds many people who were needing to be saved.

It does seem that, wherever they went, it was deliberate, and they were to make decision as to what they do based on choosing to do good or to do harm. Then, after each task unknown to them, that they were placed right back to whatsoever location or state that they were previously located, perhaps only in their thoughts; maybe?

Is it any *"WONDERING"* then, that; having proven her kindness after several jumps and have saved numerous of people from dying, that she was approached by her ATD
(i.e.: Advisor Trainer Director), mentioned in chapter 27?

And having satisfied to her obedience, that she was given her GA orders, whereon she became aware of herself, and of her various task, where-on she was progressed unto the duties of a Guardian Angel.

So, if your spiritual eyes are peeled and are open, at some random points you may observe an unusual figure or the figure of a female, and it seems that each figure wore the backward CK-broach made of shiny yellow gold.

It also seems to be that (until Charli-Alice had satisfied her given tasks and prior to her GA progression), she could not recall any memory of what has happened or transpired with each transfer and may not or could not decide whether she was able to repeat the same locations, or places whether she had been. Maybe yes, maybe, no?

The last thing that was remaining with her memory was that she is on a train and is trying to get off. She didn't even know that she was no longer alive and without her assigned human host body after so many Earth years have passed. To her, it seems the same time frame, or day that she needs an exit fare.

However, once she was progressed to GA duties, her memories became intact and granted her permission to access every person (humans) as by her assignments.

She was also able to move beyond time, space and dimensions without restrictions

THERE TO BE FOUND AT ANY TIME OF FULL MOON:

Corresponding with the times of mysterious appearances; consistent with each full moon when it's bright and hanging low, was usually the time best predictable when it may be possible to anticipate and to encounter this phenomenon.

One who means no harm to anyone, but rather to help or assist or save someone from their plights, anguish, dilemma, and sometimes the first on-site, where assistance has been needed.

She is more like that of a modern-day superhero, but one that is really trying to be identified, but it seems that no one is acknowledging of her mysterious and random appearance.

<u>The things to understand is that:</u>
    (A) The world is a very big place, and she may not have been given assignments limited to only one region or country.

    (B) For anyone to see her, she would have to attach herself to someone who has just died or dying, and this is still unclear.

(C) If a person is still alive, and she attaches to that person you would not be able to recognize her as the CK person, or her golden broach.

(D) You may only see her if your mind was prepared for this type of encounter, and you are a spiritually minded person believing in such things.

The golden broach that Charli-Alice wore also has the letter "K" and the first letter of her supposedly her last name, which is identified as, "K" as in Kuya.

It is believed that the initials CK (broach) were meant to be her name as Charlie/ Charli- Kuya being worn on her right side, while in the norm; a lady's broach is usually worn on the left side, so it is believed.

What's more, is that; the letters are in a backward form which seems to suggest that each time Charlie/ Charli-Alice materialize on this side of humanity, it is believed that objects associated with her have been shown or viewed in the opposite order as though looking in a mirror.

Watch for her hand's movements as you might also notice that she may be left-handed, since previous interaction as noted previously when on a certain train she poured from a teapot, two cups of coffee with her left hand, as well as served a meal on the train with her left hand while her right hand was holding something else.

In most cases, a right-handed person would typically hold the tray with the left hand and serve with the right hand. Although none of these affirms anything.

If Charlie/ Charli-Alice is interested in you, she may approach you before you have a chance of approaching her.

It is to also note that she is normally moving at immeasurable speeds that she could be in many places all within a fraction of a second, and no one's eyes can see anything moving at such speeds.

However, I feel that it might be possible that because of a possible affiliation, and due to a belief, that she may have left, or attached her unborn child's spirit on me (the author); when she visited Jamaica, and when I was a Newborn, which attachment might be a reason that we might be able to summon, and urgently call on her to be present.

I feel also; that; even if that were the case, and even, if possible, that she cannot openly say that she is my GA, or even that she is an angel. Nor can she say that she is a ghost. It all goes against laws of the Celestial and Terrestrial, and even against universal laws of mortality.

It becomes us who is to determine who she is and that of faith, even as she may not show as herself; therefore, we may only realize that we had an encounter at some point after the fact or what then will be felt much as a dream and nothing else.

This might be possible, and might be something to consider, but we don't know for sure as to what may be accomplished where CK is concerned. It is the things which I had experienced over my past years, that have shown me that something more than meets the eye has always been with me throughout my life that there is still no perfect clarity.

Following this book, there are plans and expectations for several projects and developments to follow, and by then we might be much closer to being able to contact CK and ask her to show herself. But don't hold your breath, it may never ever happen, but we will try very hard.

It is a wild and crazy notion, but all that are written in this book, was from my account of this character, and my Gut-Feelings of this CK Kuya. None of this and these developments would have been perceived without these inspirations given me. Real or not, and I cannot confirm anything.

However, after proving by eliminating what are impossible, whatever remains, however improbable, and if possible, could be the truth.

There has never been any scare tactics or frightful incidence where Charlie/ Charli-Alice is concerned, thus with each encounter, it seems that she is feeling that now she was coming home to family, and friends whether she has or not, or was that the case remains questionable, however, there are more information coming soon.

From this mysterious information we have, no one knows for certain about her family and relationships. We are trying to locate!

Charlie/ Charli-Alice just wants to go home as indications seem to suggest that she might have had a tender passion, and other precious things (like her baby's spirit, her Bo) or things that are missing from her that she longs for, and cried for, that seems endless and unchanging.

SONG: [**I Cried for You, by Katie Melua,** (Katie Melua - Just Like Heaven)]

Since, and just as her golden broach, it is observed she is not wearing a wedding band suggests that she probably was still unmarried, but she may have been madly in love as is or was the case. ***Nonetheless fictional.***

No one truly knows for certain where or how Charli-Alice died, since she was stuck on a train wherein, she had no money to exit and get off the train, as the story goes.

She may have been caught in one of the fatal crashes (as is believed) and her body was not identified, and since she had no formal itinerary.

But whenever there is a transfer of souls from mortal life to death, there happens to be an opening of a portal to conduit souls from one dimension to the next. Whether this is a one way or two-way, the case or not we may never be certain. However, CK from that spirit side has found it and had entered through to this mortal side.

When so many souls are being transferred at the same moment; the portal and energy field must be of significant size; and likely remaining open for some extensive time. Being open; it may be accessible if found by someone. Anyone who is mortal, or spirit may be possible to enter.

This opening could probably be for up to as many as 40 days. Longer or shorter, but who knows, who can tell or discredit?

Over many years we have many people went missing, went out of sight and no one knows why, or what had happened, leaving no clues or trace behind. Currently in the world over, should one collect even the most recent lists of the last five years, that the list of names would be significantly very long.

STILL MISSING IN THE WORLD:

Here is a statement found on Google, Dec 2019: 90,000 people are missing. While many of them end up being found, alive or dead, many others remain missing to this day. Jun 11, 2018"

People Disappeared Mysteriously:

Found Online under:
"By the mid-1990s in the United States of America, the number of missing persons cases had grown to nearly 1 million, though this number began to decline in the 2000s.[4] <https://en.wikipedia.org/wiki/Lists_of_people_who_disappeared#cite_note-usstat-4>

As of 2014, an estimated average of 90,000 in the United States are missing at any given time, with about 60% being adults, and 40% being children;[5] <https://en.wikipedia.org/wiki/Lists_of_people_who_disappeared#cite_note-usa-5> in 2017, the total number of missing person cases was around 650,000."

Perhaps as a prime example, would be the notorious, or mysterious "Bermuda Triangle" where there remain only speculations.

Could it be, that some of those portals remain open indefinitely, or they come open during a certain period?

Could it also be that these portals may be in the air as wormholes as well as on the surface of the Earth otherwise in someone's closets or wardrobes?

Even Jesus when he was resurrected, was seen up to as many days as forty, before he was taken away, and out of sight.

Ref; the Bible; KJV; (Acts 1:3) *"He shewed himself alive…, after being seen of them <u>forty days</u>…"*

SCRIPTURAL REFERENCE OF GHOSTS SEEN:

Scripturally, you may read that when Jesus died on the Calvary cross many souls have been transferred from the other side to our mortal side, and have been sighted among us for some moments, or time, perhaps as many as forty days duration.

GHOSTLY PIGGY-BACKING:

While Charli-Alice is still trying to get home, her appearance may be shown for some moments or periods in our time.

But she cannot stay, because after crossing over the other side you may not return, at least not to stay or perhaps only to stay by assignment to piggy-back with another human to continue earthly progression.

However, Charli doesn't know this, as well as she doesn't even know that she may be naturally have been sanctioned to the place where spirits go after the body dies. But where is that; really? Who has any perfect knowledge of where that is?

It also seems to suggest that Charli may show up at various times or place since thousands of deaths are happening every second, and spirit conduits are being open and close quite frequently and at an alarming rate.

Even so, it is not quite accurate, or otherwise quite probable, that anyone can track her movements or predict accurately her appearances.

CROSSING PORTALS:

CK must-have figure it out; how to cross over at these portals, because she; or so it seems, has been sited at other random places where there were no disaster issues, however, <u>at each Full Moon</u>, it seems to be consistent with various supernatural or terrestrial happenings, and CK may be or could be seen.

Since no one has been trying to track her movements specifically until now, the record of appearance is random and very inaccurate.

Also, and since we took consideration of so many random occurrences, we feel that this "<u>Charli-Alice phenomenon;</u>" as being told, maybe real, and we are searching for the opportunity of identifying her, and maybe get a hold of; or a copy of her golden broach that is shaped as of a butterfly wings, which she wears on the opposite side of the normal.

(Features of CK's golden broach)

It may seem to have some (possibly) untold features, possibly <u>giving or enhancing</u> "<u>foresight,</u>" or much of the following list.

<u>What Are:</u>

Foresight, patience, tolerance, how to have and give love, joy, peace, to care, to bless, and much of the best of virtues.

It would also appear that Charli-Alice may have been switching forms at every opportunity of a chance of getting off that mysterious train she now thinks she is still riding.

These are assumptions. Maybe! Who knows? But don't close the book, follow us in all of the series, because all that there is regarding CK, one or two books cannot hold all of the information,

So, if your eyes are peeled, and you are vigilant, at some random point and when the moon is full, you may observe an unusual figure; or the shape of a female who wears the backward bright glowing CK broach, made of brilliantly glowing gold.

This may be your lucky day, and she wants to give it to you if you acknowledge her.

And if you did not receive her broach, then you must talk to us. Message us if you have registered your "CK Kuya, GTNE book-1 & 1a, and the GAQ book-2, i.e. following from Sept-Oct 2024.

SOMETHINGS SPOOKY

Just be aware that the gold may or may not belong on this side of the portal, and should you receive it, it probably has to be returned, and while you are wearing it, who knows what might occur with you then? Maybe very spooky!

But, and however, we will be trying to replicate her golden broach, that we may have them distributed as a part of our rewards program.

"Well did she ever return, no she never returns, and her fate is still unlearned", she may ride forever, but she's the one that never returned.

"AYUӜUYA"

Repeat: Corresponding with the times of mysterious appearances, consistent with each full moon when it's bright and hanging low you may be lucky to encounter this phenomenon.

The golden broach that Charli-Alice wore has the letters "CK" which are the initial letters of her name Charli-Alice Kuya, but when mirrored, is identified as "AYUЖUYA." However, on her broach, letters are backwards as ЖƆ.

ENCOUNTER WITH CK Kuya

Should you encounter her, call her name out three times as "Ah you, ayu, ayuЖuya" but in Jamaican it means: "It's you. Look here!" or "Look there! It's you."

CHAPTER – 28 ЖϽ

LOVES MANY SPLENDORED THINGS:

Bo had previously Met CK on a couple of brief moments, but it was Sally who sort of officially introduced Charli-Alice to Boise while they were at a Summer's night party, some time before the break from school.

The introduction was not meant as one would try to set up a connection for dating or for any hookup, since Sally and Boise were a sort of already into each other for the longest time.

They never had any discussion or an affirmative regarding their relationship.

They grew up together and have always been the best of friends.

Boise was just slow at deciding on intentions for a serious relationship. While Sally; she also never realized to the acknowledgment of her inner-most feelings for Boise. This; due to their long years of friendship, and, as they were still quite very young.

Both were free-willed spirits, quite the happy-go-lucky, and due to being hung-up in their own comfort zones.

CK came along very innocently; emitting a most powerful, beyond great effect on Boise, not able to resist her natural; and effortless charm that triggered; and sets off his hormones, sending a boy's male characteristic on the hunt.

LIFE-CHANGING ENTRANCE:

At a certain point in our life, and at some undeserving moments, we are blessed with precious gifts that; at times leave an impact that is recognized as something quite monumental, and indelible that will never ever fade away.

As CK entered the party-hall; though not trying to impress anyone specifically, yet Boise Jangles nearly fell to her feet as he beheld her figure upon her entrance.

Glazed with passion and a desire worth dying for, Boise finds himself trying to tame what seems to be something gone wild inside, that he never knew was there, now eager to break free trapped there inside his chest.

Interestingly enough, Sally was dancing with Boise quite the nonchalant fashion, when finally; she spotted Charli-Alice as she walked further in.

Gracing the party room in quite the majestic and royal fashion that matches <u>the silky violet-blue color of her dress</u>, that spoke to the bouncing jet-black and natural curls of her hair.

Yet; Sally had not noticed or realized that Boise's eyes had already left their own place of birth.

They had been splashed and pouring all over CK's model like broken water-balloons, as only at a mere glance, and in a distance that nearly floored him to his demise.

Finally, they said their hellos and were happy greeting each other at length and acknowledging their away-ness from the life of school, classroom setting, of books, broken pencils, geography or the Cheerleading club.

It was Sally who first complimented CK about her dress. Although not crazy expensive, as those of Sally's; who; or her parents; were of plenty more pockets of green than CK.

Although not super-rich they were not, however; could afford more things for Sally as her demeanor demands, being the oldest of her other siblings.

while Boise quite the inexperienced; when it comes to complimenting a girl's attire and fashion, agreed with Sally's comments about her dress and added, "You are so beautiful tonight."

And no! It really wasn't the dress, but the figured contour of outlines, and a provocative silhouette of Monarchy that looms under, as a roof begs her pardon; for not providing her with red carpeting whereupon she may be introduced.

WEARING EACH OTHER:

While Boise; was so moved and intrigued by CK that he couldn't help, but to be thinking nearly out loud that; "he'd love to be wearing her on every shirt that he'd ever owned;" even from here forward, and likewise; her wearing him on every dress and attire that she wears going forward.

Boise had never seen CK dressed in any formal outfit before, and how stunning she was, as though she was born the way that he was seeing her now.

A dress that changed her appearance from the girl at school only seen in school uniform, and yet not every day, as he was going on two years older than CK.

Said Sally, "Charli, oh I so love your dress! It is so you!" "Thank you, Sal!" CK responded quite modestly! She wore an outfit that is to be described later on, and for a number of reasons.

Sally continued; "Did you just bought it for this party?" "No! I had it for a few months now, my dad had bought this for me when I was getting ready to come here to school,"

By this time, she had not yet hit the age of sixteen and probably just shy of it.

While Sally had already gone past that threshold and had blossomed under Boise's inexperienced help, and probably part of the reason they were sort of together at the dance and sort of into each other.

Naturally, Sally then introduced her to Boise, and they chat for a while and before you know; it was mmmm! awesome! between Charli-Alice (CK) and Boise Jangles, and that's how it all started.

It should also, be noted that this introduction was actually the third time that Boise had words with CK, even though Sally had no idea that they met each other prior to going to this party.

For those reasons CK quickly warmed up to Bo which led to their first dance together.

SONG: [**The Tennessee Waltz, by; Patti Page**]

Now, CK had no idea that Sally and Boise were sort of into each other and have had some romantic relationship previously.

CK doesn't know them quite to that extent, and whilst Sally and Boise were not officially dating, and neither one the boyfriend or the girlfriend, yet they were quite that close, that, had they given it some thought would have realized their potential for such a relationship.

Something happened passionately between Sally and Boise at some previous moments, and while in the heat of that moment, so they remain very good friends going forward, and since he was her first on the sexual matters, and vice versa (V.V.) too.

PASSION LEADING THE WAY:

After this third meeting with CK, so it seems to take off from there.

Boise just could not keep his mind off CK. They; to the most part have constantly been in touch.

They have been to various places on dates and have communicated quite frequently to this point.

Their passion for each other was through the roof as the ceiling did speak to CK, and told her that the skies have no limits, and no restrictions to sour.

They spent lots of quality time at various parks, shows, movie houses, games and so forth. Their relationship was very rich and strong.

JAMAICA - MASSACHUSETTS – USA:

While CK did not have a sweet 16 birthday party plans, she was invited by Boise to spend the day at the Jamaica Boat House and Botanical Park of Massachusetts, USA.

CK had no ideas of what to expect since she had never been to such a park before, she had never been boating until Bo took her out and showed her how it's done.

CK had never been to many parks till she met Boise, and this one is the one very special park that she won't likely to ever forget.

"Bo!" She called his name. "What are those tall yellow flowers way over there? Are they Sun Flowers? I have only read about, and seen in pictures?"

Boise responded, having taken a moment to reflect at the name she called him by.

"Oh! That sounds so romantic hearing you call me like that. No one had ever referred to me like that before."

"Is it ok to call you by that name?" CK asks.

"Oh Yes! Yes of course. And yes, those are Sunflowers. There is a great patch of them there. Do you want to go there and see?"

"Oh, for sure!" CK exclaimed, followed by the provocative next question. "And why would I not want to go and see after coming so close and with you?"

Boise: "Ok then young lady, let's take a run over there then." Said Boise.

Challenging her ego, and at the same time stimulating a rise in her blood flow, that now began a heated rush to rapidly distribute a number of the feminine emotions, hormones, and chemistries to an already elevated measure, when a relationship towards romance is on the rise.

CK: Yes! I'll race you there.

"You're on!" said Bo.

"Oh! My God, they are so beautiful, and so tall."

Bo carefully popped off the prettiest of the flowers, so very gently, and then very delicately placed it in CK's hair.

OMG! She exclaimed under her breath. When he touched her hair and lightly tickled her scalp from his touch, did someone asked; was it raining, or is it my imagination? I must breathe eeeasy as her thoughts are all over, while she struggled to maintain her composure.

With each progressive action, they embraced as they carry-on through the park; and at each change, stage and range (CSR) increase their blood flow and anxieties.

This, because their hearts continue to sense that, they maybe they were still running, when in fact they have actually stopped to be smelling; as it were Rose's along the way.

"There you are, my princess," said, Bo.

"Your Princess?" CK queries as she chuckled.

Oh! If only Bo knew what he has begun? Or; perhaps he is learning.

But, by lightly parting and preparing her hair with his fingertips, allowing his roaming, probing forefinger's intimacy to delightfully penetrates her hair so as to locate the best spot in, and near her lubricated part in her hair.

That too; by the sensations he was creating, generating, arousing, and transmitting, I had been told; could, and does have a tendency of waking up some very vital emotions in a girl's, or person's anatomy.

Thereby, his gentle positioning, settling her head with his already rigid fingers, and installing the hard end of the Sunflower's stem between her now prepared hair parted, that to a great "*WONDERING*" that CK was able to be still standing through that moment.

Her heart now became truly confused, and still bewildered by the reasons, why so much blood flow was required to be flowing to a more central location on her body if she wasn't indeed still running? Blood should have been more proportionally distributed.

(Boise's Remarks Good Job To Compliments)

"Yes! And you look amazing, so absolutely amazing CK!"

"Thank you, Bo!" responded CK with a gentle affectionate kiss on his cheek and Bo blushed for the first time, and he was lost for words as he seems to appreciate and acknowledge her affection for him.

He never saw that coming and he couldn't speak. His heart drummed at his broad chest and he *"WONDERED!"* What is going on inside, and where the drumming is located since it sent ripples all across his chest and made him feel vulnerable.

A cold sweat broke from his forehead and not because of the sun or the heat of the summer.

His palm sweats and a feeling of sudden momentary jittery came over him that he had not felt before nor could he speak due to the lump that subdued him; and that which was blocking his larynx.

For a moment he was taken away as if to a different place in time. A place of bewilderment and beauty.

He was now seeing a different glow all over and around CK's face and her feature, standing there with the most beautiful smile and aura if only he could see, or truly feel what had overtaken her.

By this time the placed sunflower accenting the light shade of pink under her light skin of color at her cheeks. As for her eyes, they truly glow that Bo now "*WONDERING*;" was she truly a star? or was she a miracle?

"Bo! Are you alright?" CK asked. "Am I alright?" Bo repeated her question and answered. "Yes! Yes of course." Making up some excuse and trying to justify that it was nothing.

Even CK did not realize the spontaneous effective ability that she suddenly developed by this one person.

It's as though a "WONDER-Woman" she became. From that moment on, it seems as though a love spell was placed on Boise Jangles perhaps never to be broken and yet unintentionally.

They walked for a while and come up to where there were ducks at the pond.

"Here! Let's play with those ducks. They are so many of them here."

Bo: "Oh CK, be careful they have young ones and may chase you to protect the chicks."

"No, they won't!" CK assured him.

Bo: "Just watch out for the Drake, let's move gently and not to startle them."

CK: "Which ones are the Drakes?"

Bo: "The Drakes are the father ducks, the big ones with colors on their heads like that one," pointing to one of the males nearby.

CK: "Oh! Look at those babies. They are so adorable; if only I could pet them."

Bo: "No chance here! Not allowed."

"What about feeding them?" CK inquired.

Bo: "We could! But we don't have any grains."

"Do you know why ducks fly in a V-shape?" Ask Bo.

CK: "I have seen them flying like that before and often wondered why, but it never matters so I didn't inquire further."

Bo: "When they fly in the V-shape it makes flying easier, because they don't create extra wind resistance for the ones behind."

"Awesome, even birds care about each other. That's so sweet."

"Look! Bo, in the water on those stones are small black turtles, many of them here.

They even stand on each other's backs."

"Yeah! They do that too when they are mating."

CK: "Booo!"

"Sorry, I said that." Bo apologetically.

CK: "I WONDER! Why did you think of that now? Was it because of that little kiss?"

Bo: Blushing again, answered, "No! Not at all." CK knowing that he was lying, but let it slide.

As they walked along there were some musicians just sitting and playing as musicians usually, do in some public places for tips and changes.

Bo walked over briskly and talked with them and walked back towards CK who was otherwise occupied with something in the park.

"CK," he called for her attention, "let's go and listen to those musicians for a bit."

"Bo, you play the guitar maybe you can join them."

«Ha! Ha! He chuckled. So; they went over and sat down.

"What's your name, young lady?" One of the musicians so randomly asked. "Charli-Alice" she replied.

"Ok then Charli-Alice, my name is James and here is a song for you."

That moment was a good time, so Bo; then reached into his pocket and pulled out a little gift that he'd brought along for CK. He gave it to her and wished her, "Happy Birthday CK!"

CK; being astonished by the unexpected gift; had no words for a few seconds. And for those few seconds; many thoughts raced through her mind worth discussing at some point.

Then finally, she exclaimed; "Oooh! Bo! Thank you!"

Her eyes quickly bounced back up towards Bo's face, him being about five inches or so, inclining her hypotenuse that was towering above her.

Her, being some five and a half feet of pure attractiveness, that flourished with poise and grace, enhanced by expert hairstylist and facial provocation to the arousal of masculine desires.

Eventually, she inquired; "may I open it now?" "Absolutely; he exclaimed. It is for you. Remember?"

CK anxiously yet gently, timely, carefully unwrapping with delicacy as though stretching time; not wanting the moment to pass.

Finally, after breaking through the ties, and sifting through the protective packaging, CK now arriving at the core, where once more; decked by the pains of surprise and gratitude.

Thus, she exclaimed, "Oh; my; god!"

Definitely a TKO once placed in that ring to be challenging young Boise Jangles of Massachusetts.

Upon beholding the content of her gifting package, it sends a glow from her gift itself; reflecting in her eyes, she's now exuding appreciation breaking from an inward to an outward sense of emotions, then with an exclamation; "oh my god! Bo; this is awesome!"

Boise; reaching over simultaneously, "let me help you with that."

As he most gently, very timely, with extreme tenderness, and intimacy, but carefully proceeded to attaching CK's now cherished, a lady's golden broach. He was placing it just to the left of, and slightly above her now insanely affected bosom, that she was rapidly being aroused.

While by this time, her eyes are as though a solid rod iron connecting her eyes to his as she pierced her way through and into his entire being.

Hoping that there should not be any end to this moment of Ecstasy that is winding her up like a toy made to operate after fully wound.

Boise, although being careful yet he is still clumsy, and quite inexperienced with handling ladies' dressings, which now is innocently causing the fire to be burning hotter than flames.

That by seemingly accidental, yet not really, as he was being extremely subtle in trying to awake what he feels may have been sleeping. His hands are now slightly touching, brushing, and tingling the promiscuous of the <u>"oh my god"</u> in her speech.

Finally, Boise had her broach pinned on and said, "There you go!"

Even while they had company, and while the musicians played her "happy birthday to you" song, she had no shyness any further, took hold of Boise's neck and with a real kiss this time, she kissed him and said, "thank you."

Well! It was time to push on. Boise dropped five dollars into the can of changes that the men had laid out on the little park table. "Thank you" said Boise and CK simultaneously, as they went on.

CK now walks with her head leaning on Boise's shoulder while with her arms; one holding Bo's arm closest to her, while her other arm now wraps around his waist implying a sense of belonging, as they walked along together.

They were very quiet for quite a while not saying a word. I suppose digesting we must digest after feasting on things that brings us to such highs in our life.

After walking for a while, Bo finally asked, "do you want to go paddling on the water?"

At first, CK might have said; no thank you. But now that she has been brought from a place of cold and frozen solid, to a now quite melted, very steaming hot, fluid, and still melting on him she was.

This could also mean that for each step she made, she was feeling, and hearing the liquid swish even down to her shoes they were so wet.

And anything that Bo would have asked of her; the answer was certain to be an indubitable yes! At this point, he could do no wrong where she was concerned.

<u>SONG</u>: [Cruising, by; Smokey Robinson]

Boise purchased the tickets for a rowboat, and they went inside and out on the water.

He; quite so romantically paddled, and paddled, and for a while they enjoyed the graceful movement with not much to be said as they were both trying to tame the urges that is associated when two persons are passionately touching even in the slightest way.

Many times, we feel as it were needles and pins that should hurt; but why does it suggest pleasures.

Having taste of a first kiss that now exchanged some body fluids between the twain does leave you wanting for more.

The sun was hot, and their interest was not about paddling and rowing any boat anymore.

CK was not interested in anything else but to be comforted, and she most definitely needing Bo's help before she faints under this kind of pressure. Even If she wanted to faint at this point and time, her desire was definitely not for the glaring intensity of the sunlight what she was needing.

Although that played and contributed a small part, it was not helping her current situation, now that she has come to this point in her life.

Finally, their eyes met again, and as it were very strong magnetism had pulled them together, and as intense as the sun, so begun their kissing that was so long overdue.

Kissing that went on for some time as they were communicating within their own selves and making responsible decisions inwardly, when finally glancing into each other's eyes as though for confirmation and permission, when CK responded first, verbally, and quite audibly to the affirmative.

"It's ok Bo, it's no problem whatsoever, I want this." So; without further hesitations not even thoughts to look about for spectators; they found themselves flung down on the floor of the boat.

"CK;" Bo was about to further confirm when CK interrupted and said, "Bo; it's ok! I promise!"

SONG: **[I Want to Know What Love Is, by; Foreigner]**

CK was not really sure; if Bo had done this before; or not, but he was two years older and must have, CK thought.

Not like her, she had not done it before, and at first, was a bit scared, but because she became in such a physiological heat and fluid, that her fears were not an obstacle, or that to make her nervous about her first-time sex.

They both were extremely excited, anxious and nothing was stopping them although awkwardly it seemed.

Boise remembered things he had heard from his friends, and from what he has seen in movies, etc. Pertaining to lovemaking and sexual intercourse techniques, as well as this was not his first, but second after over one-year passing.

Before too long he was into her, and she moaned with the passion of first-time penetration, and of it all.

Although painful it felt at first, yet the passion camouflaged her first-time sexual discomfort under the blazing sun-heat that also brought the extra sweat to cool her face.

Extra sweat also brought to other parts of her exposed skin, and elsewhere as she melts, and flows fluidly under his weight, his awkwardness while pumping, and pumping to the dept as never reaching before.

By this time the boat was really rocking and swaying as the intensity mounts higher and higher.

It was surprising that someone had not seen and called 911 to rescue someone from their ecstatic passion that seemingly became out of control.

While, for the first time, their hot and passionate lovemaking, coupled with synchronized coterminous climax shot off simultaneously where pain meets passion as never before felt, or experienced in their entire life and for the first time.

Surprising too, that, because their passion was so hot, so intense, and in combination with the Sun rays and heat, a "<u>WONDER</u>" that there was no smoke from the fire that they lit up over the water and inside that small boat.

CHAPTER – 29 ЖƆ

LOVE HURTS:

It is now 1955 and Boise J., CK's one and only true love, continue his search for Charli-Alice who is still nowhere to be found.

He is badly hurt, broken hearted yet he continues his search however, wherever, whenever he can.

SONG: [Love Hurts, by; Nazareth]

However, there is but one thing he has: going for him. He also has a friend (Sally) one who would do anything for him, and who was hoping that Boise Jangles (Joey) would have eyes for her, that perhaps he would consider taking her for whatever he desires of her.

SONG: [If You Can't Give Me Love, by; Suzi Quatro]

She (Sally) has been there from the beginning although she knew how much Boise (Joey) loves Charli-Alice (CK).

Sally tried with several efforts, but because she does not wish for Joey to be hurt anymore and perhaps turn it against her.

Sally, in most cases stayed clear, yet from time to time would have visits with Boise and Charli-Alice (CK).

Whenever Sally had asked Boise over to her house, he always went along with CK. Because he knew that CK and Sally were also friends; so, he never thought anything of her going along. However, Sally was always burning up inside whenever she was there with him and yet pretends that it was ok.

There was on one of those visits to Sally's place when Charli-Alice (CK) told Boise that she (CK) was going to visit her mother in another city; and will be gone for a few days, so Sally knew exactly of CK's plans and thought to make up her own plans as well, that must coincide while CK was out of town.

Some days or few weeks even, after CK became missing, that friends and relatives felt that she died at some point in one of those train accidents, possibly where bodies had not, or could not been identified, and so they held vigil for her.

It is a belief that there was even a private funeral service held for her after some while, but young Boise Jangles refused to believe, thinking that she ran away from him on account of his behavior towards her, blaming himself in a very grave way and so ran off.

Boise's friend (Sally), has always had a special desire for him, wishing it was her that he is so madly in love with.

However (Sally); trying to comfort Boise (Joey) saying that; "Alice is gone, but I'm still here", and that she (Sally) knows how to help him getting over Alice.

<u>SONG</u>: [Living Next Door to Alice; by; Smokie]

Sally was also waiting that Joey would ask her to be closer than just friends, now that Alice (CK) has been gone for quite a few years by now, but Boise Jangles (Joey) could not. He loves CK too much.

By this time everyone who knew CK, felt much love for her somehow, because of who she really was and for the very same charm that Boise saw in her with each time he laid eyes on her.

Everyone in her neighborhood has missed her and became very sad because of her disappearance and fear she might have died somewhere.

SONG: [Sad Song Say So Much, by; Elton John]

For all those years of searching for CK, Boise (Bo or Joey) has had nightmares and frights, because it seems that CK might have been sending him dreams, and also trying to reach-out to him.

It's now all the way into 1977 and more than 27 years has passed since CK went away, and Sally continued to waiting in the shadows for the day when Boise J. (to her he was Joey) would consider her, and to start looking at her with a different eye, so she cries for him, especially since she never really made a family of her own with Boise Jangles, her Joey.

Also, that's because she too was, and still is so very much in love with Boise (Joey), while she lived a life of sadness without the man she so truly loved in secret, and who could be the father of their son, or more children.

SONG: [What about love, By Heart]

This time Sally sat down with Boise (Joey), and thus the words came straight out so suddenly as though, like something was simmering for a long time that with the slightest opportunity something was bound to happen.

"Joey!" she said! "Haven't you any eyes to notice that I am always looking out for you?" She asked.

"How many times have you been drunk, blacked out, became suicidal and nearly killed yourself, whereas; it's me you call on, and I came to your assistance and brought you home with me?" "Joey!"

"And Joey! How many times have you counted?"

"Yes! I know, Sal, I know, I know that you have always been there for me, and I am so grateful to you for everything Sally." Joey replied.

Sally continues:

"But Joey; I don't believe you really knows this at all. Why else do you think that I am always hanging around you so much? All my F-life for you! For you! For you Joey!"

Sally now crying profusely saying further.

"Nobody! But no one else but you Joey, and what do you do? Still chasing after some dead girl after nearly thirty years gone. You're chasing after a ghost Joey! A ghost for God sake!"

"It seems to me that you are so very, very clueless, and that's because, after, …"

Sally paused, with tears in her eyes she continues.

"After nearly thirty years have gone by, and you are still believing that you are going to find your Charli-Alice, your sweet little CK, and bring her home again; after she ran away from you, and then what? Then what Joey? Where will you take her? Where will you go and live with her, even if you did find her? Then what?"

"I know how; that you don't like to hear what I have to say regarding CK, but let me tell you again, she was my friend too; but she is gone! Gone for good, she is dead! And she is not coming back Joey." I am here for you all those past years, and you are depriving me, depriving us of what we can become together for all those years."

"I have saved up money, and I do have a place, my own place, and I've made something of myself Joey while I waited for you."

"What a fool I was, I could have had any other man I wanted, but I was so blinded by love for someone who had but a child's love only; not knowing what to do with a real woman, one who was so madly in love and over the mountain for you, and only for you; no one else Joey! I loved only you!"

Sally still crying, drowning in her tears of sorrow and grief.

"So why don't you get smarten up for once and look around you so you can decide, and help me to stop from hanging in the shadows, hoping that you will for once look at me like you did so many years ago, at our first time we made love Joey? And even as you still don't even know what we had; that we had…"

Sally hesitated, she stopped her talking and cried more. Joey (Boise) still had no idea what Sally was trying to say about what they had between them.

Sally continued: "Joey, you were my first; and dammed near be my only, and I have waited this long for you. It's time you let go of CK, she is gone Joey, gone! I am still here for you.

SONG: [Meat Loaf: Two out of three ain't bad].

Joey on the other hand could not, and insisted he will find his Charli-Alice someday. Thus, he continued his quest still declined on settling down with Sally.

CHAPTER – 29-1 Ӝꓛ

SALLY'S RAMBLING

While Sally rambles on yet does not realize what this is doing to Joey. His pain was as it were; by a long 6-inchs nail driven into his pain spot he is for years trying to remove, but by this time Sally had somehow extended that nail-length times-2, counting what she had done that drove CK to running.

[But did she ever return? Yes, she has returned, however, her faith is only partially learned to this point, whereas now she's reassigned as the GA Charlie-K, for doing much more than riding the rails of Boston but not as one of the Charlies who never returned].

Then suddenly with massive aggression that seems by a *'Thor's hammer'* now have violently taken a swing to have rammed and staked that (now 12-inch long) nail far deeper into Joey's pains that had him reflecting on moments previously spent with CK at oft-times and prior her disappearance.

Now he has found refuge where he hides himself in the memory of CK, that while Sally continues with her rambling, Joey now able to find CK that now he is able to transfix himself into selective memory-moments where now he is able to always find CK in his thoughts that seems quite and more real than not at all

If only he knew that CK knows where he is and had been reaching out to him, trying profusely to gain his attention to no avail, due to a stubborn mindset that locks out what his abilities would have allowed him, but to what has now deprived him.

Now, for all the years that CK has been trying to connect with Bo, perhaps by him tapping into his memory to escape current day's multiple disappointments and of Sally's badgering, that just maybe, he might be able to free his mind sufficiently, to then consider questioning; 'how has he been able to escape those ***'what could have been'*** during his life?'

Just like the times he had attempted to hurt himself due to the various points of unbearable hardship being so alone, tired, hungry to the point of starvation, or damn near froze to death. Otherwise, so hot that found him no place worthy or affordable for him to clean or cool himself.

Those or where it seemed he could go no further.

Then found he a place high in the sky next to an open window only to find that later it came to him that someone saved his life that day and then again that night and days that followed.

Boise then flips and wound it backward to reflect more with inspiring, reminiscing memory-rollback. Triggered by Sally's arguments, he now contemplates on the times he had spent with CK, when he had the most fun as it seems that those days could not have any ending

But only now, while Sally continues… and with words saying, *"bla bla bla!"* then she dropped words saying:

"Joey, can you just stop, stop for a moment and think."

[But those words just sent Joey further back into his mind to the memories of CK, that now it seems he's hearing CK voice what she had whispered so long ago with the similar tones saying, *"Bo, wait stop stop! Miss Jones miss jones! Miss Rubberneck Jones sticking her neck out again and watching us!"*

SONG: [**Miss Rubberneck Jones**]. (By Titus Turner)
https://www.youtube.com/watch?v=SW0ap3YF94A

But then it was just two days later that we met Miss Daisy Jones at the market and then she didn't seem to be such a bad lady after all. For she said to me and CK,

"I often think of you two as a very wonderful looking and nicely matched couple." Then she added*: "Are you officially dating?" For I often see both of you together and so close together.*

Both CK and I simultaneously replied with a very strong blend of assurance and trust, *"Yes mam we are!* Then CK just looked at me and to her then said: *Thank you mam for saying that!*

Well, you know kids, I really didn't mean to pry, but since I might not get invited when the time comes; so, if you don't mind, I want to buy you both a soda as it pretty hot today. Do you mind?

We looked at each other with "Shock & Awe! Like really! Are we hearing right? Then with a polite pretense of gratitude saying, thank you Miss Jones for being so kind!

Then I interjected; We weren't expecting… But before I could complete my comment she interrupted. Don't mention it!

Thanks again Miss Jones!

So, we were left alone to enjoy our sodas, but we could not let this go for a moment then to question. What had just happened? Was that the same **Miss Rubberneck Jones** we know? And CK started giggling ever so sweetly as though from the sweetest song of a songbird. Then I hugged her and we re-hugged each other with no further wondering or concerns about MRJ.].

CHAPTER – 30 ЖꙄ

HERE I GO AGAIN:
<u>SONG</u>: [Here I Go Again, by; Whitesnake]

Boise Jangles is on the search again for CK.

After some time of reflecting and contemplating, Boise decided to take a trip towards St Paul, Minnesota.

He recalled that he first seen her there.

<u>SONG</u>: [Big River, by; Johnny Cash]

BO QUESTIONS OF CK'S PROFESSIONAL INTEREST:

Although CK had said that she does not believe that she has relatives there, yet Boise having been to many states and cities in search of CK, and not found her, he feels now; that St Paul may be a worthy place to start over his search.

Charli-Alice was also a very bright student of the similar grade standing as Sally was; but seems quite the opposite of Sally's demeanor. Just different they were and yet both very unique. He searched his mind for the type of places what would attract someone by the type of person they were, and who might go to the places of interest, or what type of jobs would suite a person's character and skills.

CK used to be a B+ to A student rating in her grade 12 equivalent classes. Her rushing away happened in the late of 1949 to early 1950 and he now "WONDERED" whether she had gone back to finish her college studies, and what profession she might have gone into. With this unknown makes it difficult to even imagine the field of her interest, or work category she might have gone into.

"Well! Where can I go next to look for CK?" Considered Boise.

"St Paul hadn't blossomed; so, don't expect any catch there, I better make my way on down to that next block."

And so; with a familiar dryness in his gullet, he winds up on down to the port of davenport, where to make his next stop, maybe to have himself a fav-of brew where some old farts perhaps weren't so drunk and noticed someone familiar.

Hopeful and optimistic; Boise now walked up to the bar, and with a pitcher to the rim did wet him a whistle and did it far from slim, then carried on drinking till someone wounds him up all over again.

After a while, came a fam of a voice, one he hadn't heard for a number of years passing.

"Hey there Boise! How did you end up all the way out here? It's been a while, and aren't you a long way from home?"

The voice exclaimed as Boise turned about with a surprising grin all over his face.

"This is my guitar picking friend James from Massachusetts. Do you still play?" "Yes-a-do! A man's gotta earn a little bread here and there, don't we?" "A reckon we must, we must!"

Replied Boise J.

James commented:

"But aren't you a bit far from home? How did I manage to run into you here?

Last time I saw you, you had a little running with you young lady. How is that going now? Are you here with her?" Inquired James.

Boise responded with:

"Tell me, have you seen her James?"

James fired back at Boise:

"You know! I thought I saw someone like that girl a few days ago and I thought of you, though I am not sure since I didn't speak with her."

Boise:

"Oh my god! Which way? What did she look like?"

"Well, this time she held a beige lady's purse and was dressed as though she was going somewhere, more like catching a transit or, but she walked towards the ferry dock."

"Thank you, James, Boise said and attempted to go off on his search when....

"Whoooh there stallion! This is late in the evening, this is no time to make any start out, all places are closed so you may stick around and have you self another drink before you go. Start this in the morrows instead at night suggested James.

Boise anxiety level soured and he lost all sense of planning, but then after being counselled came back to earth and said,

"Yes! You are right and I will think about this tonight and make moves early morn."

Boise hadn't slept a wink the whole night and was up very early to catch the next ferry by 6: AM and be off to inquire about, where possibly she went.

From the description he presented, he was told that someone fits that description, bought her ticket for St. Louie, and wend her way.

When last he picked up what he thought to be her trail, followed it on down to Memphis, and then he lost her. This time well, it seems losing her all over again and he's getting tired.

SONG: [That's How I Got to Memphis, by; Tom T. Hall]

Well, he didn't stop there, and so he has gotten down to Baton Rouge, on the river queen,

Then surfed on down to New Orleans, and like the same old; same old shooting a blank all over again.

In as much as Boise will try, and try, and try, yet he will never find exactly what he is looking for, but anyone who will persist will eventually find something, and not necessarily what they are searching for, but will eventually find for certain.

Searching can be a good thing, and searchers search to find; however, can never guarantee if they will find, what they will find, or if at all they find, but by searching; one learns, develops and increase in patience, which in essence is a virtue, and one of pertinacity even doggedly and patiently. That is; if one held fast to patience long enough, and without caving or imploding.

(The Positive VS. The Negative)

In searching, a searcher needs to be prepared for the unexpected results. Not so much that one is planning and looking for the negative results.

However, it is like offering legal counselling saying that;

(One Must or Need to; "Know Your Rights!")

However, it is by the knowing of things not of one's rights; that one truly becomes aware; and knows how to choose that which is considered as the right.

One may look for the number of "twelve" but it shows up as a "Dozen", which is the same, but what were you expecting to see?

You may have found it, but will you recognize what showed up?

Will it surprise you, or will you be expecting any form of results?

What will your reaction be?

CHAPTER – 31 ӁƆ

I CRIED FOR YOU - WHY CAN'T YOU SEE ME:

CK has since; had some training and so came to realize a lot of things:

(A) That her train does not exist
(B) That her crying is not real, as she is a spirit and does not have access to most of those human capabilities, or emotions as were possible while being hosted
(C) She also realized that there is no ground that she stands on
(D) Time does not exist for her
(E) There is no day or night, no sleep required and no pain or sorrow existing
(F) That her movement is not subjective to measurements
(G) That she may slow down her rapid or hyper-movements so to be able to attach or touch objects or persons, to possibly be seen by the human eyes to some degree, and able to interact with humans who are somewhat prepared to see spirits, sense or communicate with spirits to some levels. Some just don't have that ability, or that they are so distracted that even if they have the abilities; may never able to break free from their distractions so that they may see the spiritual things.
(H) She also realized that there are so many more things she is able and capable of doing as a spirit

(I) That she never realized before, that because she thought that she was still human being, but now she is able to do things from a spiritual aspect and mostly what she wishes yet limited to things physical even spiritual

(J) That also she may not yield to temptations, and are still restricted by terrestrial and celestial laws that she must abide otherwise will be subdued by created angel beings specific for those Laws enforcement

SONG: [Why Can't You See Me, by; Concrete Blonde]

From her training and various realizations gained, CK has since seen Bo, but Bo's eyes are not prepared to see on those levels. CK is trying to communicate with Bo, but Bo cannot see her, at least not at that moment or as yet.

Well it took some effort on CK's part then finally their eyes meet only for once and no more, Bo is too distracted. However, CK still rest with him and even sleeps with him wherever he ended up, drunk or not and with each effort that CK tries hopefully for Bo to see her has failed.

SONG: [I Cried for You, by; Katie Melua]

CHAPTER – 32 Ӝꝯ

HOW BOISE J. MET CHARLI-ALICE KUYA

It was only about a year or so; after their first encounter, that Sally really started thinking that she should be with Joey. By this time, he had already fallen and confirmed to Charli-Alice regarding his desire for her, and so she became his girlfriend. It had been that way for a while, until he erred. He then, from guilt; tried blaming CK that drove her away, even though they had plans of getting married, as well as one being on the way.

Bo met CK while he was taking music lessons across the street from CK. But thought he'd met her prior in another city, but don't recall exactly at this time.

She had not been long moved into the neighborhood that summer and then started going to the same school as with Bo, the fact of staying in the same neighborhood.

It was the morning break at school and Bo noticed CK in the hallway at school and recognized her as she just walked out from her classroom into the hallway.

SECOND MEET UP WITH CK:

"Hi! Hello there! I am Boise!"

While showing off his very sporty kind of macho walking style being 17 going on 18 at the time.

"I recognize you! You were the new girl just moved in the house across from my house, aren't you?"

Amazing smile on her face.

"Although, I also think I had seen you somewhere before, can't remember for sure, but I did say hi to you a couple of weeks ago just before we got back to school, right?"

New girl: Yes! That was me! Yes! Of course, I remember, and I think you, you were just getting back from your guitar lesson from the house close by.

With a bit of a lazy frown on her brow of a descriptive charming wellness all-round, and a sign of thinking it back and rewinding the memory reel for an affirmative.

Boise J: "Yes! Yes, I was just practicing with my friends. We are talking about; someday we will start up a band."

"I am Charli-Alice!"

With her right hand outstretched, followed immediately by:

"But my friends call me CK." "Alright! CK it is then! I'll call you that. CK! Ok!"

Boise J. now having a flash-back moment, the type that is prominent when two soulmates have senses, felt or a simple skin touch of each other and one that forever holds them together with unbreakable desire as an assurance, that they are for each other and for no one else.

Soulmates are the couples that stays together for life as only they can cope or endure each other, no matter the case, scenario, fights or by any existence of the above, they can never be broken from each other. It is only soulmates that can become one afterlife and no one else.

Regardless of the several other mates one may marry, it is only one that belong and can spiritually bond together through the afterlife to be one and the same with male & female combined.

"Say, do you have folks down in St Paul, Minnesota?" "Oh, I don't think so, but I was visiting there a little while ago."

CK: "So, what will you name the band? Do you have a name already?" She asked curiously.

Boise J: "Not really. That thought is really fresh right now."

CHAPTER – 33 ӜꙄ

IF I CAN'T HAVE YOU

Well, some questions have been asked of Boise Jangles (Joey), comments were made, and parting words were exchanged especially by Sally. So, about the last time that Sally had words with her Joey and told him, rather ask him: "Don't you want someone to take care of you?"

<u>**SONG**</u>**: [If I can't have you by, Yvonne Elliman]**

DON'T YOU WANT SOMEBODY TO LOVE:

Well, I feel that that was the question finally started the ring-thru to Joey, even though slow at coming around to the realization, that the chance of finding CK has become very slim.

Finally, years have gone by, and Sally finally stated her last resort ultimatum, not waiting any longer. Joey started to reconsider; that; perhaps he should act on taking a partner since there is no sign of a chance that he is going to find CK after searching for over 36 years. He was 19 when CK ran away and now cranking the clock chasing his 56 yr-old on the horizon.

Sally had been there for him each step of the way in his search for CK., and as a side note; it should be mention that they had two previous encounters in prior years, which to Joey's ignorance; one of those encounters produced a son that Sally was afraid to mention or to shed some hints with Joey, who continues to be in the dark even to this point in time.

The chance for him finding CK has diminished to nothingness, and his lost love has not left him any clues whatsoever, and not from the get-go. At least none that he was able to identify though CK did dropped numerous of clues, hints, obstacles, other persons encounter where from a spiritual Biggy backing was clearly unsuccessful.

Sally's son for Joey; although unknown to him is quite the grown up now, and never met his father nor was he given his name.

Sally and Joey were both virgins, still very young, being 16 and 17 years of age. They were beginning to explore those avenues when it first happened. Sally couldn't wait any longer for that reality, and Joey at 17 seemed overdue.

Then at the second time around, this action was part of the reason Joey's became angry at Alice and part of him trying to save-his-hide by guilt-trip!

Ever since Joey was a little laddie he had this passion to ride the trains and as he grew further into his teen years he would just hop on a train and just ride for the entire day before heading back home.

His mom would get upside his head because she worries about him naturally.

Boise might have influenced CK towards jumping onto a train; as that's what he was intending on doing trying to wash away his guilt, otherwise to take some time and figure out how to deal with his infidelity at this early stage of their relationship, hence the reason why CK ran and hopped into one such train and never returned.

"Well; did she ever return?" Umm!

There was no riveting connection when Joey and Sally first made out and hit it off, but they remained the very best of friends over the years, except that Sally hid her true feelings for Joey, and she never told him that she was hoping that they would be together, because of what was some sort of pride I suppose.

But now?

<u>SONG</u>: [Take A Chance on Me; by; Abba Band]

Sally never mentioned her desires and feelings for Joey, because he was already head over heels for CK, hence Sally; disappeared for a while, now sheltered by Mother's comforting and helpful nest.

<u>SONG</u>: [You Can't Hurry Love; by; Diana Ross & The Supremes]

Just prior to Boise getting angry at CK, he was with Sally.

Sally needed to maintain that friendship; hence she planned it that she would become pregnant with Joey's baby, wherein at this point she went away and hid from Joey.

When she delivered it was a son who was not given Joey's name at birth, and the child who probably will not come to know his father, as well as his father does not know that he; intern has a son.

PREGNANCY TO HOLD HIM:
(The Grit of it All with No Stones Unturned)

Realizing that CK was out of town and probably not returning for three days, therefore Sally set out with the courage to try and win back the man of her long-time dreams, by whatever means necessary, or with whatever measures she must measure and could dream up.

As a last resort, Sally did not care, even though she knew that CK was already six to seven months pregnant with Boise's baby and not married.

Having counseled by Mother dearest, who has been the Matchmaker for so many years, and while Sally; now strong enough and determined to use whatever power she possesses, to gain his affection, Love, or attention, to be drawn away from the love of CK.

So, unlike the first time, Sally, this time; planned it so very well, that she even went as far as to ensure her ovulating and her egg had been dropped.

CHAPTER – 34 ЖƆ

AFTER MANY YEARS JOEY RESORTS TO SALLY

Ring, Ring, Ring, Hello! Hello!
Hi Sally! this is Joey" (Boise Jangles, to Sally; he was Joey).

"Hi Joey! Where in Gods earth are you?"
Sally exclaimed vehemently with a very extreme bewilderment.

"I've been worried so much about you, where are you?"

Joey struggled for what to say to Sally.
"I, I ah! Well, I...."

<u>SONG</u>: [Joey: By Concrete Blonde:

<u>Sally</u>: "Joey what are trying to say? Where the hell are you?"

<u>Joey</u>: "Are you home now Sal?"

<u>Sally</u>: "Yes Joey! I am home now."

<u>Joey</u>: "I will be there in half hour ok?"

<u>Sally</u>: "But Joey, are you alright though?"

Knowing how he suffered so much already Sally needed the assurance that Joey was not in any kind of issues before letting him off the line.

Joey: "Yes! Yes! I'm alright Sally, see you in thirty."

So, Joey hopped on a city bus and headed to meet up with Sally.

Joey: Anxious and nervous at the same time since it's been a while since he had spent any quality time with Sally.

It seems the norm; that he would call Sally to bail him out of jail, or assist him out of some other unkindly situation, considering the ongoing investigations for the disappearance of Charli-Alice, or where he might have passed out, or fell, due to drunkenness, and she had to rush over and assist him from his awful plights from time to time.

This will be different this time around, and Joey is now so high with anticipation on romance instead of the latter. So, after many years have passed now Joey is really looking forward.

When they were young, full of fire and their years were ahead of them, it was "*WONDERFUL,*" and they had some great times.

Sally; back then has been a very gorgeous, beautiful, bright and tall legged individual in high school and into college.

The type who had an enormous compelling influence on most peers and intrigued all the boys to take a second or third glance, as well as everybody wanted to be her friend.

When it was time for having fun, she was always the life of the party, made everyone felt loved, and insured a good time at all events and get-togethers.

She was considered as being smart, astute, and knew just when to exit so that she does not accidentally or otherwise end up under some boys' influence, or under someone's bedsheets for any ecstasious moaning display, or other unwelcomed abuse or worse.

It was when finally; her 16th birthday rolls along; that she decided that she was not losing this opportunity of allowing young Boise to take her down for her first real sexual episode.

I supposed her life and growing up with Boise had already staged this impending outcome in so much that; when the time was full and Jupiter was in her favor, with Cupid rooting for her, making it happen was inevitable and a no-brainer. But were they soulmates?

It was after this amazing and unforgettable event that she first began to refer to Boise Jangles as "Joey"; in short for his last name.

Even by so doing didn't prep or make him be any wiser or be aware that she desires and wanted to be more than just his friendship.

Most definitely she was the dancing queen, and she sang almost as well as the future group of Pop vocal artist.

(The Leading Cheerleader)

When at scarcely fifteen she joined the school's cheerleader team where she shortly after a few games was promoted to be the leading cheerleader.

Oh! Such attention she could draw to the team, and yet boys could not glance away from her every move but retained their gaze which was at this time welcomed, since each gaze was due to a professional, and no doubt by an invitation.

But that's what cheerleading is all about, isn't it?

When at seventeen it really clicked that she desires to be with Joey, but she now blames herself for introducing Charli-Alice (CK) to Joey, because now she is indubitably blocking her progress with Joey.

Sally now found herself wanting and pushing on to eighteen turned to her mother-dearest for counseling and advice as to how to win back the man she is in love with.

SONG: [Someday We'll Be Together: by; Diana Ross]

After counseling with mother dearest, the crafty hat went on, and Sally lunged forward to win back her man, or so she thought anyway.

This dying or otherwise desperate act was the sole reason that had triggered a series of negative chain reactions and thus altered lives, started a new unplanned life conception, caused sadness, hurting, tears, fears, and thus spawned hatred, and anger as well as the lack of positive progression in their lives. Then of all that followed that affected joey's life and where it got or sent Charli-Allice to never return. But did she ever return?

Charli-Alice had been out of town and went to spend a few days with her folks in another city.

Sally knowing that CK was not around, had plenty of time prior, so she concocted a scheme and tricked Joey to an evening out, and especially knowing that she had dropped her egg and started ovulation, making this prime time, and one that must not, cannot fail.

Joey trusted her and never planned on any making out social; being his long-life and best friend beside CK, but when under Sally's spell he was not able to see such deceptive voluptuous enchantment coming.

An enchantment that was so powerful, that when coupled with a few strong shots, the right measure of tantalizing men erectile potions mingled with the late teenage testosterone, against dim lights with one of the most beautiful bodies one has laid eyes on, no telling how far the night moves or could extend.

By the time Joey realized what had happened three days and three nights had already passed at the whims and spells of Sally, leaving him completely dry. Sally had taken it all from him.

Joey finally became fully aware had to now be on his way to meet CK as previously planned.

"Sally, I've got to go." "Really; really got to go now!"

"But Joey we need to talk and have a conversation this time because a lot have happened, and things are different now Joey. So please hear what I have to say, will you listen? Joey my love!"

"No, Sally!" "I really need to go; like right now!"

Sally knowing exactly what she had accomplished was proud of herself, and happy that she made the only move she could towards winning her prizes.

If she couldn't have her man, at least she feels deserving if only a piece, or part of him.

Realizing now that Joey must go, she pretends to be crying with the hope that Joey would be happy, and wanting to spend more time with her, but things took the opposite turn.

SONG: [Sad Eyes, by Robert John]

When face to face with CK, it didn't take two moments for the female intuitions to realize that something was not right. Things was not the same as before.

CK: "Bo, what's wrong my love? You seem very agitated as if something has frightened you badly."

BO: *"Where have you been all this time CK?"*

Bo asked, as if accusingly, or something like that.

"Did you go back to an old boyfriend?"

<u>CK</u>: *"Bo! I'm pregnant! Why are you talking like this? I told you I had to go and see my mother, as I was not feeling so well, and because I am only about eight weeks left now from delivering." What is wrong with you?"*

Bo now threatening to leave on the next freight train, but instead of waiting for him to go, CK made the first move to the train station instead of Bo.

A LEAP FORWARD - Boise Looking Back to Sally

After some years have passed by of unsuccessfully searching for CK, that Boise had all that time for thinking and considering as it concerns with his age and health.

Bo had not realized what damage he might have caused, by allowing Sally to trick him so badly that sets him on a path in searching for his true love and soulmate, as now a leap into the future shares how his life may be impacted with no finding in sight.

Boise arrives at Sally's place, knock, knock, knock, with some moments waiting while he took the time to view the scenery and reflecting on days gone by.

The neighborhood setting and residential landscape does sort of reminding him of the place where he and Sally grew up together.

Joey was mentally exhausted, drained on deciding his next move, whether he should go here or go there, and after years of going nowhere, it became a standing still for Boise Jangles to now turning to Sally as a last resort.

Having seen it all, with all things there looking familiar; has brought him "WONDERING" to himself; "what else is there to see or do?"

Having looked everywhere with all patience and pertinacity, with just one hope, that is to find CK, so that he may finally have some peace, rest and forgiveness, yet he turned up with nothing, at least not yet, as he is still hopeful in finding something in the end, or before the end.

CK Kuya's QUOTE:
"Looking For Twelve – A Dozen Came – What Were You Expecting?"

Realizing that he wasted a whole life and have gained nothing, nothing whatsoever which had begun to be leading him to contemplate whether he should climb the highest place he can find for a steep-drop, or find the deepest river, or ocean where finally he may be hidden underwater from the contentions in his mind, tormented by voices in his head saying, "Have another beer!"

Guardian Angels do work with every person, regardless of who, or what we are, or what we are doing. It also seems that; they for the same results may be saying the same, or similar words to many people if those words were effective even as they were given to the songwriter or artist for these songs mentioned herein.

SONG: [Someone Saved My Life Tonight, by; Elton John]

He never could realize the passing hours that seems so endless; as he is haunted with the chanting of a slip noose; hanging in his darkest dreams, strangled by haunted social schemes four o'clock in the morning.

When with strong mindedness or shaken out of his sleepwalking episode, and then his thoughts came again and it seems as a trend when someone has been contemplating or tempted to suicide and the thoughts seems the same as by the song writer who sings: "Saved in time, thank God!"

And: "Someone saved my life tonight! hypnotized with those sweet freedom whispering into my ear. You're a butterfly, and butterflies are free to fly", or I would have walked head on into the deep end of the river, but someone saved my life again."

CK FINDS BO:

What Bo J. has not realized is that CK knows now how, and where to find him and each time that he tries to be suicidal that he was each time saved somehow by his loving CK as she always watching over him.

She at times leaving him clues that he just never picks up on. Many times, she would drop a white feather about him where there was not possible for no birds to be there in as much as to dropping a feather.

Other times he would hear like his name being called and there was no one, or that a chill would suddenly come over him and other random occurrences would happen that he would have noticed; but never attempts to try and figure out.

He is still left with no answers, and the only thing he has remaining and that which fueled his daily life is this one positive thought, that he promised himself; "to never giving up, whatever the cost, or pain, or expense," until he has found, and have seen an answer that provides him with some hope. Thus, again he turns to Sally.

Came the squeaks of a door handle and the creeks of being open.
<u>Sally</u>: "Oh my God, Joey it's you!" (Sally always calls him Joey). "Hi Sal!"

Joey greeting, and Sally; in-turn gave him a great big hug. "It's almost ten years, maybe more; I don't even remember now."

"Where the hell have you been"? "Good that I kept the same phone number, I knew you would turn up somehow."

<u>Joey</u>: "Yes that's right."

"Come in Joey. We have a lot to catch up on." "How have you been Sally? I think I am doing alright Joey." Sally replied.

<u>SONG</u>: [A Song for You, by, Ray Charles]

<u>Joey continues:</u>

"Sally, I've been a real jerk, and I've treated you badly and very unkindly over the years. You've been right all from the beginning. I know your intentions of me is what I hope to be, and yes! I've treated you badly when there was no one more important to me besides you."

"Oh Joey, no!"

<u>Said Joey:</u> "You kept me as a precious secret with nothing but truth, sharing everything with me. You make everything clear, but I was hiding." "You have been my greatest friend since we were but children, and I will remember all this for life."

Sally broke down and cried, worried and felt sorrow for Joey, and concerned for how he will go forward from that point on. Sally knowing that she is the one fully guilty and responsible for Alice's death and for ruining Joey's entire life, because not spending a life with one's soulmate is all but a ruin to anyone.

Look around from country to country, from state to state or city to city then from street to street and notice that for everyone who is without their soulmate (male and or female), potentially ends up this way otherwise, if not on the street found themselves in somewhat various predicamental situations.

SALLY BLAMES HERSELF:
With tears in her eyes said:

"Joey, what's done is done. Now, are you hungry? Cause, you're making me to cry again, Joey. I cried enough tears for you already, and I blamed myself for what you and Alice went through. If I didn't seduce you Joey, Alice my friend, would still be here, and you wouldn't have to go through all what you did trying to find her.

REFERENCE TO CK'S BABY
"Also, too that, you and Alice would have had your lives going on together, even as she was very soon due. Joey, I blame myself for interfering and messing up your life. And this haunts me every day of my life for all these years, and I have tried to be there for you with the hope of some form of compensation to you was the least that I could do."

"Yes! I know Sally. I know all that too."

Sally: "Now are you hungry?"

"Well, actually I could have a bite."

I was not prepared for company, so why don't we just go out and get lunch downtown?"

"That sounds fine Sally."

Sally: "A city transit will be coming along in about ten minutes, so let's go and catch that one, and then the train downtown. There is a lot we must talk about Joey."

SONG: [Thank You for Loving Me, by; Bon Jovi]

While riding the bus Joey recalled previous bus trip back in the days of schooling, they must have been eleven and twelvish.

SONG: [Maybe it was Memphis, by Pam Tillis]

Joey: "Sally, do you remember that time we did a field trip to Memphis?"
"Oh yes Joey! That was the first time we actually had a real kiss you and me, not counting the many small ones you stole when we were very small."

While riding the 2:50 with Sally towards downtown, all that Joey had been searching for, after so many years has just passed by him as he beheld what he was looking, hoping to find, and yet has not recognized CK as she passes so close to him till she has disappeared.

She has been trying to make herself visible to Bo for all this time, and finally their eyes met. but she is still not experienced enough, or yet, on how to reach out to him. One thing is for sure she is never going to lose him again.

Joey (Boise) was sitting in the aisle seat of the train while CK walked by, looked at him squarely in his face and smiled as he returned the smile briefly.

But then, when CK ran away from him she was 17years old and after 36 years she has not aged, and Boise was not looking for a 17-year-old young lady.

As she passed by and for the split second it took for Boise to realize what he had just seen, finally turning around with a sharp twist of his neck nearly gave him a bad whiplash, followed by his upper body and to his second surprise, found no one whatsoever walking in the aisle.

For some moments he was not able to speak after that for a while. The one thing and hope he was searching for, he had just found and seen yet not believing.

They went for lunch, and he could not order what to eat, could not eat from his tormented mind and punishment of what he knew he had seen, or not seen, and yet seen and he knew it for certain, however; could not speak of it, or say this to anyone, thus he had entered a state of denial.

"Joey! Snap out of it! You look as though you had seen a real ghost."

Said Sally, who was quite concerned, having seen a different side of Boise (Joey). While Boise at that time still could not say a word. It was as though he had completely lost his abilities for uttering if only one word and remaining in a state of shock and awe all that time, but more like in the musical tone of a base chord, being Looo.

<u>SONG</u>: [Needles and Pins: by Smokie Band]

After a while, Boise beaconed to Sally, he wants to go from that place. "Ok, Sally, can we go now? Still not able to speak.

CK had been trying to find the ways and means how to reach out to Boise, since she has learnt some things about herself as a spirit, and the powers she possess or otherwise gaining.

She still knows how to love by that emotion, and she still desire to be with Bo, perhaps just to be able to see him, or him seeing her would be enough, but it does not work that way with spirits. Nor is it just black or white either and certainly not that simple in her secret life.

Sally: "But Joey, you haven't eaten anything at all?"
Boise (Joey); finally coming around, said, "Yes, yes I know, but its ok I swear. Can we go now please?

Back at Sally's place:

Boise (Joey): "You know Sally, I've been thinking, but it's very hard for me to find the words to say it out to you."

Sally now suspecting perhaps what Joey wanted to say, and about the reason he went to see Sally, but knowing her own situation; decided to speak her case first, so that Joey may not go to that thought, whereas, since that would just complicate, and might make matters worse for her, than it already is.

Said sally, "Joey, I am finally getting married in two months, I couldn't wait for you anymore Joey I'm sorry, but I will always love you, Joey!".

"He is my daughter's father and a very good man.

"What is your daughter's name?" Asked Joey (Boise).

"Her name is Ginger; she is in school now."

Sally did not mention her son to Joey as questions she doesn't want to be asked or to answer would be forthcoming. However, at some points in the conversation she mentioned that:

"But Joey; I could have also given you a son, and you would have been my son's dad."

Sally had mentioned this perhaps as a little hint that still did not work out for Joey, and he still does not know about his son.

"Joey, it will be a very small wedding and is what I now wants, not the big one that I was hoping for and with you Joey but will you please come to my wedding? I'm inviting you now since I didn't know where or how to reach you before. It is good that you came now and not after."

BOISE IN HIS MIND:

"That is not what he was hoping for!"

And because he had seen it all, had been there and now repeating here. What else? What more could he not endure? As the thoughts race through his mind, finally he responded to Sally who was already "WONDERING" whether Boise had reverted to another kind or case of shock, and again not speaking as before some minutes ago.

"Sure, Sally! I am very happy for you and yes! I will come to your wedding."

"But Joey, I am still curious as to what had happened back there on the train this morning, can you please tell me?"
SONG: [Katie Melua - In My Secret Life]

O Sally, yes, something I believe I saw, but I am not sure, but for all those years I have looked for CK, I thought I actually saw her on that train, but that person looked about the same features and age of CK when she first went away. But the craziest part is after she pass right by us and I turned around there was no one walking in the aisle behind us at all.

Sally: "O Joey that's insane. Just let it go." "Yeah! That's what I thought you'd say and why I couldn't talk about what I know I saw for sure."

Although Joey didn't have much to go on, yet he managed to find himself a second hand suit and now planning to be all nicely dressed up for this very special day and occasion for Sally, which he had recently begun to hope for, but was too late on deciding as usual, until someone else came along and took charge of what was being held in store for him for many many years until he lost it all.

SONG: [And The music played, by Matt Monro]

After the wedding, perhaps this was to be the last time that Joey and Sally may be seeing each other.

Boise Jangles. Now turning 66 years old and spends his time around a familiar gin joint bar when a certain journalist writer came around and he was happy to share some thoughts on life.

SONG: [Watermelon wine, by; Tom T. Hall]

CHAPTER – 34-1 ЖꝛƆ

CH-34:

Said sally, *"Joey, I am finally getting married in two months, I couldn't wait for you anymore Joey I'm sorry, but I will always love you, Joey!"*

THE LAST TIME MARRIAGE CAME TO MIND:

CK KUYA RESIDING HOMETOWN & HERITAGE

There was a period known as the ***"Era of Migration"*** prior the 1940s" and well beyond the 50s, that by 1949 between July to August Charlie-Alice Kuya (CK) had already turned 16 and barely into 17th year of age when she met Boise Jangles.

Since we are following this development and trying to trace Charlie-Alice's origin the various dates mentioned as well as potential ethnicity, heritage and such are but assumptions, due to points of events we've found as being consistent with the various trends.

We invite our readers to follow along with the progress of our findings that perhaps we together may locate the family of CK for further information.

JAMAICA PLAIN:

From the early 19th century, Jamaica Plain often referred to as being ***"The Eden of America"*** for more reason than one. This region was also recognized as one of the greenest neighborhoods in the city of Boston.

From the description perceived of CK, seems to suggest that she was of interracial conception. Hence her hair was long, shiny, jet black and mildly with natural curls, which seems to suggest as not an origin of any one particular nation, but a mix of a few.

Her skin tone and colour light, fair in complexion and with all things put together does gave way that one is compelled to take a second and third glance (all from the author's inspiration), through gut-feelings and from where the source to this story seems to derive as well as from the fictional derivatives that give meaning.

She was largely interested in the **Performing Arts** and theater, but while not a great dancer or performer herself, yet for some reasons her interest was naturally observed as one for TPA.

Along with the *"Era of Migration"* and people shifting, that wherever the people went, their culture and forms of entertainments went everywhere with them and like footprints in the sands remains as an indent and a brand that does not fade or vanish but is left behind as it was impressions cemented there permanently.

JAMAICAN MENTO ENTERTAINMENT:

There was a new form of entertainment and dance started in the Caribbean (West Indies), known as the **"Mento,"** which was developed and originates particularly from Jamaica to Boston and elsewhere during the great **"Era of Migration."**

This Mento entertainment (with its Triple Threat Discipline in the Performing Arts) depicts **"Acting, Singing & Dancing"** and has introduced, even inspired the various unique moves.

- Some specific dance moves which then challenged the entertainers, Rather that the entertainers did; and still does challenge the entertained guests to participate.

- Even till this twenty-first century day and age, those moves such as the 'LIMBO' dance is still being enjoyed wholeheartedly! (Getting down and dirty, bending over backwards to the lowest that one thinks they can).

- At times people takes pleasure in just spreading legs to the widest they feel to expose, thus emitting sight pleasures to the crowd of other viewers who were (some) waiting on their turn for bending over backwards doing the limbo to the lowest possible, while sliding and inching forward in jump-stepping glides; progressively under lowered bars according to the rhythm and beats of the music and until they've passed under an ever-lowering horizontal stick-bar, till at times can seems quite exposing or even erotic!

- It however seems that everyone seeking for such types of entertainment still feels the inspired urge to challenge their own personal ***'Body-bend'*** to the various moves and songs-lyric stimulation.

- With songs such as those in 'Mento,' they still do inspire the various moves with compelling energy and entertaining lyrics of songs such as those listed below.

JAMAICA CULTURAL MENTO SONGS OF THE PERFORMING ARTS

https://music.apple.com/us/album/jamaican-mento-music-hits-1952-1958/504182429

Searchable in YouTube:

- ***'Limbo limbo, limbo like me!'***
- ***'Linstead Market & Day O!'***
- ***'The Jack Ass Song, (Donkey Bray)!'***
- ***'Banana & Breadfruit Season!'***
- ***'Iron Bar!'***

Just to name a few…

CHAPTER – 34-2 ЖƆ

THE INSPIRING BO TO CK's QUESTION

When asked of CK, by Boise Jangles (BO), *"What is your favorite hobby?"* CK replied; "TPA & IP!" While Bo is like, "What's that?"

CK responded saying, "The Live ***Theatre Performing Arts*** & ***Interactive Performances***."

Bo: "Do you mean like the circus with animals and like *'Merry Go Round'* and such?*"

CK: Mocking, jokingly! ***"Bo; haven't you heard of Broadway theaters for acting, singing and dancing?"***

Bo: *"Sure!"* *"But I never heard that much for the acting part, but for music and singing…"*

CK interjecting said; *"Which of course is part of the performing arts! So, you see, we do have some important things in common; aside from just …"*

Bo: *"Aside from just what?"* Asked Bo, but CK responded: *"Oh never mind!"*

Only now, Boise never wanted to leave well-enough alone. It's not in his nature. That comment from CK alone kept him asking, which then brought out the playful insisting and playful ***Performing Art of***

Stimulating' a loved one to some sort of perceived sensual passion, where delicate romancing begins.

So with some playful response where love grows and inceptions are marked, does suggest that; *"Hey! I know where you're at now!"*

Those; 'I know where your stimulative points are located', and by what means they do (such as with a tickle, that tickles to CK's giggle sensors and rib-sides), are just below her armpits tickle-spots and to where sensitive emotional sensors protrude or extend-to the sides.

Whereas to be tickled is unavoidable to be touched that trigger arousal. Thus; when two people are so much in love and tender-spots are encountered there is no telling as to where this will end up, where the night goes or leads to?

Thus; came an outburst from CK's surrendering, suddenly yelled-out: ALRIGHT! ALRIGHT THEN! *"I meant we are more connected than we realize."*

Bo then confirms with a reply, *"Yes I know!"*

CHAPTER – 34-3 Ӂꓛ

JAMAICANS MIGRATION FOR WORK AND OPPORTUNITIES:

During the 1940 and into the 50s many opportunities became available, and people were shifting globally. Thus, In Boston, the town of Roxbury it seems quite a few migrants from Jamaica (the Caribbean), had migrated to that region and lived southwest of Boston where this community was named after the Jamaicans in due of their fondness for the Jamaica's white overproof rum.

It was said too; that they preferred to drink the rum plain. That was probably because; the assumption is that; the natural heat from the alcohol seems to convert to body heat, which also assumed to provide some sort of insulation or body-shield against the winter months in northern countries.

But for the summertime, it's just plain love for the effect of the alcohol! As well as; for some it's just their way for life that is to always be drunk based on their various life situation. Why else would someone wants to be drunk!!!

Hence the name ***"Jamaica Plain"*** was adopted.

PER:… AUTHOR BIO SEGMENT …
["Similarly, I grew up in Jamaica, born and raised, where; at ten years of age (in the early 1960s), my parents also had a small business which includes a typical 'Rum-bar' off-shooting from their small grocery store. Many of the

community folks did enjoy this Jamaican white overproof, raw alcohol drink. They also drank it 'Plain' just the same."

However organic and made from sugarcane the rum is! Yet, I personally feel that it's the refined blend of what a 'Moonshine rum' is and my wonder to question, just how the people could and can drink so much of this alcohol day after day without totally destroying their digestive system. I mean, some have died from this drink I presume, but it's not definitive as to be the cause of death, but certainly a contributing factor, no doubt!]

Jamaica Plain, MA., has since became famous for its greenery and is referred to as the Paradise of America.

*[**Spontaneous Celebrations** refers to both a building in Jamaica Plain, Massachusetts, United States which acts as **an arts and education centre**,[1] and to **a community group** which is based there. **The mission of the group** is to create **a cultural life through the arts**, and especially through **seasonal celebrations** in Jamaica Plain and Roxbury, Massachusetts and education.[2] **Its classes emphasize dance**, stiltwalking, trapeze, and other circus arts.[3]]*

Well, since CK did not grow up in this city and community of USA, Boise then Invited her to one of the events held as an annual bash, that usually takes place in the summertime. CK was excited that they do have things of modern entertainments close by.

Well, that was happening in just two weeks, and someone became overly excited that with gratitude; kissed Bo as two people in love usually do without any hesitations or the cares of anyone being nosey such as Miss Rubberneck Jones of whom CK and Bo now have her approval.

It is now realized that during the great migration period from Jamaica in the Caribbean, that CK's folks may have also migrated to the State of Massachusetts, in or near the Boston area of America and cannot be quite far away from Jamaica Plain.

Her hair was long and jet black, which suggested that although fair skin she was, she was not the typical black from Africa, although obviously mixed, otherwise multiracial she was and with the Black genes, hence mildly curly hair.

PER:… AUTHOR BIO SEGMENT …

[*The latter then seems to suggest that, for the reasons mentioned that I (the author) feels that I've been visited by CK on multiple occasions since I was little, along with the fact that my grands and great grands bear this similarity to CK and was also from east India by mother's side and an ethnicity in Jamaica known as "Indo-Jamaicans.]*

As Boise had noted to CK and regarding the upcoming annual event in two weeks that now CK is with immense anticipation, for then this would mean her first live such event and one that depicts a culture belonging to her heritage.

Although it seems she was born somewhere in the state of Massachusetts with her folks does seems to have originated from Jamaica, in the Caribbeans, yet she had not ever participated in such public events prior, nor had she been invited previously.

Well, how the time passes by quickly!

Jukeboxes were most popular from the 1940s through the mid-1960s, particularly during the 1950s. By the middle 1940s, three-quarters of the records produced in America went into jukeboxes. CK was not aware nor was young Mr. Boise J. But to their surprise came their first sight and experience of acknowledging the jukebox form of music.

CHAPTER – 34-4 Жꙅ

THE SOURCE
[find: following the final chapter]

☆ == ☆

CHAPTER – 34-5 ӜƆ

TOWARDS THE JUKEBOX ON STAGE:

The community has started coming together by 5:00PM. The annual event is largely anticipated to those who knew about it, but to a barely 17-year-old previously sheltered teenager she had no idea regarding what to expect, except that her Bo had updated her.

Said Boise to CK:
You've only been here in JP (Jamaica Plain) for like just over a year, so you've missed last year's event.

==

Reference Included in chapters as:
NOTES OR FOOTNOTES FROM OTHER OBSERVERS **(FFOO)**
https://landscapes.northeastern.edu/harmelin
k-arnold-arboretum-franklin-park/

Walking from Jamaica Plain to Roxbury
Cities, Landscape, and Modern Culture
Per existing information: That people have said.

Bo had by this time met up with CK per their previously set agreement. They wanted to spend some quality time walking the park as CK was quite fond of all that was to be enjoyed at the various parks, especially with Bo.

They wanted to walk the scenic route through the park while everyone was very much heading to the ever-anticipated event and no one cared for the park by this time.

That too, and since by the event's conclusion it pretty much will be dark by then and not the best time for enjoying the remaining Sunlight and warmth of the day when it will be time for rushing home as anticipated by everyone.

She wanted that as well; since Jamaica Plain was very famous for its greenery and paradisiacal likeness to what tranquility should be like with many shady and cool spots in the blazing heat of the summer's day; there to be had and much ahead of the soon approaching autumn season.

To CK it had also seemed and felt that tranquility can be absorbed in similar manner as with water to a pretty dry sponge, especially when that sponge is also quite dense that takes more time to absorb the pleasant rushing in one way and out the opposite or retractive way as depending on which side was turned up and down, side to side motions.

That too as though savoring was like wine tasting by the swishing from side to side for really allowing the buds to passionately and slowly, gradually identifying what palette is deserving and the effect of romancing that sponge by the rise and turns, allowing the absorption gradually, side to side or axially.

Then, with a bit of fingering, gentle squeezing, massaging, assisting and allowing the moisture spread to the ever dryer sections of such a desiring receptor, till eventually the oozing out through the various sides or points begins to happen where overflows take place and acknowledgement to satisfaction wherein sponge is by then fully saturated begins its relax-moment meditatively to finalize savoring just what pleasant satisfaction truly means.

So now and as with CK, because she felt protected and safe alongside Bo, she was very much assured that nothing could go wrong ever, when he was at her side.

THE ONE WAY WALK:

Explore this 3.7-mile loop trail near Jamaica Plain, Massachusetts. Generally considered an easy route, it takes an average of 1 h 23 min to complete. Well, CK and Bo did not need to walk all that way as they had also planned to hop on a transit for the rest of the journey.

CK'S FIRST LONG WALK WITH BO

An important aspect of this walk was to venture into the unfamiliar with CK.

THE JOURNEY OF THIS WALK AS EXPLAINED READIY BY OTHER THIRD-PARTY SOURCES:

["The starting point is at the end of the Orange Line, easily accessible from Northeastern Campus and near popular attractions like the Arnold Arboretum.'[\.\d\u]..']

Those various attractions of the entire stretch of connecting parks were what's on CK's mind being such a fascinating community of Jamaica Plain (JP) and its surroundings, however; she was also distracted, even largely attracted by the unavoidable charm ever compelling gentleness of young Mr. Jangles.

IT WAS ALWAYS THE MENTIONED AS FOLLOWS THAT: *(FFOO)*

["To walk this route was with nothing less than or short of a sense of adventure." "That over the course of this walk you will explore a historic farm, two links of the Emerald Necklace, a small cooperative garden, cemeteries, and more."]

So it was inspiring for her to agree to walk with Boise on the way to the event which was just to be casual and not requiring any formal dressing. Hence to park walking ahead of the event was appropriate they thought.

FROM THE VARIOUS WRITERS & COMMENTATORS: *(FFOO)*
["Think about how each of these sites is connected to the greater community and is influenced by history."]

This JP history is also largely connected and influenced by the Jamaican people of the Caribbean and largely so because of their cultured inclusions as have been said by many writers and commenters of this community.

It was also for the historic layout and design fascination that CK was largely interested to see for the first time, and since by this time there was no school and studies to be concerned with during the summertime, so why not; especially when you have the perfect escort?

Jamaica being tropical with lots of Sunshine and greenery that CK had never seen, so the closest to the culture and art of the Caribbeans presented at JP was to be as a precursor to miss Kuya's visit to the upcoming event of the day there to be found at Jamaica Plain Park and communities, as was also to be largely appreciated.

Now when a desire is sparked by the spoken or written words describing to one's interest thus, and per the human nature that seems to say; "I have to see what these and those are talking about."

THAT HAVE BEEN SAID AND WRITTEN BY COMMENTORS AND JOURNALISTS:

["Consider the idea of green spaces as a unifying force in the community, and how their permanence in the landscape is protected by social organizations such as the former Elma Lewis School of Fine Arts..."]

That of so many talks of fascination from landscape to artistries, lush greenery, enchanting walking trails and the ambience of hardly to be found within a park, that even when one had no cares of such muse must indubitably become enchanted when found to be in such a place, nonetheless.

Now these parks were by far and wide the talk around town, the various communities, in the newspaper and in the school's classrooms, hallways, dorms and by so many words of mouth talks in conversations that had gained CK's attention.

Whereas now she needed to experience for herself. Well, if a chaperone or a guard for her body was what she required, well she did pick the right person and for what else that comes with Bo.

Their plans to the park did include for a rest time, as a long walk was indeed anticipated if one was to get through the parks if you were not one for hiking.

Well, their stops were but quite a few and for many different reasons which cannot be said without some romancing in the park. At certain stops they'd inscribed their names on the various trees with the hope that should their path lead them back to those various places and trees they'll observe whether their names grew larger with those trees.

Well-being alone in a great big and secluded park during a time when the most of the patrons are but few and where there was nowhere to be found the likes of miss Rubberneck Jones, and that too being alone with the most attractive young chick in all the schools that Boise now felt quite privileged and in his mind had some plans for touching and kissing then to see where all that would extend to.

After much walking it was time to take a well-deserved relaxed moment and to have a snack and drink.

Well it did not take much time to locate one of the best and nicely shaded, even seemed privately located hideaway spot where one could chance for something beyond just walking, talking and even eye-balling to observe the ball of beauty as it were a gift wrapped and have been handed to the likes of young Boise, as it were a pleasant birthday gift.

One that was most certainly arrived with a plan as to be cherished for a lifetime.

Otherwise, as long as the durability of the gifted item was, or of that which was at one's grasp where there seems to be minimal resistance that could hinder what was rightly very ripe and meant for the taking.

When it had seemed that now was the time for such a move, it then became obvious for certain required words for directing the conversation to where permission should be granted by those channeled words, but could he find those words?

Well see, Bo himself had sisters too and younger as well, of whom he was very protective and by default being the older brother he had to be. So, where CK was concerned he knew he had to tread lightly making no mistake that could hurt his demeanor and protective characteristic.

Well time is at the essence, and it was not to be wasted, because then it soon expires and relatively so fast when no progressive, even positive movements are taking place.

By this time, Bo's fingers are getting the idea that; hello; we are waiting! Feet are taking turns in tapping the ground as to hint to the brain saying like; maybe we should move closer for as a start don't you think!

Well those suggestive did bring some ideas to Boise's brain and also due to the fact of his eyes becoming dilated and found to be somewhat lost as CK had by now bent over; forward for preparing to share a snack and drink that she'd brought along.

At such an opportune moment eyes had fallen well within the cleavage of her bosom and seemingly got completely lost; even so much that fingers got talking again, pushing with nerves ending persuasions.

The thing is that; fingers have no idea regarding what consensual means and that you can't just touch people's private places without consent or invitation. Even if you had accidentally dropped an item in such a place. So, hello! Give us time you think maybe!

Their excuses were that eyes became lost, that fingers wanted to reach in and retrieve eyes because eyes by themselves could not return to sockets without the ever-assistive fingers.

Like what would we do without fingers? They inquired. Just think! It's a no brainer, they commented.

Like boy you need us! It is us that brings you pleasure and satisfaction day in and day out. Who do you suppose that does the squeezing, touching, feeling, caressing, massaging, fondling and so much more for you?

But then Boise now has an added and very crucial problem, that while eyes are seeing sensual pleasure spots and lost between cleavage, fingers are anxious for reaching in to rescue eyes lost and for other reasons besides work.

Feet can't keep still from this constant floor stomping and clutching of toes with spine and muscles are getting tensed as they prepare for something sensual and where veins are becoming expanded due to the rapid in-rush of plasma for transporting extra oxygen and the massive requirement of the driving force of testosterone to the various areas, now calling for energy and power to keep up their designed for specific duties; at specific moment or time.

Well they don't know any better, they are just and only doing their jobs.

This then feels to those complainers as it were, like someone had just pushed or pulled on some switch to turn on the ***'Emergency-Fire-Alert-switch'*** that beaconned the shrill of an announcement; ***"Make-Ready-Team' an emergency is at hand!"***

The thoughts of sensual opportunities are the culprits for initiating rapid blood flow. Which then sends the sound of an instinctive voice like command that seems to say; Hellooo! There is something happening down here. It feels as once before, as then it was great, but I'm choking here now! I need some relief! Kindly do something soon because I'm curled up and squashing!

CHAPTER – 34-6 Җꗾ

THE UNWELCOME FAMILY & 'THE-MOMENT' DISRUPTOR

Well, the time had swiftly slipped by and CK had not been aroused. Sex was not one of those things on her mind, that due as one of principles she had been raised and lived by.

To the moment that Boise had now been very well pressurized in so much that his body parts had been terrorizing him he had then began to make a move, but to his undesired surprise that had just happened to 'hop-along Cassidy'. Well, what do you know, ***Daamn! He exclaimed profanely.***

No one had told them to watch out for any critters that are naturally nocturnal or for that which could so easily disrupt what he had hoped for and at such a most opportune time and most convenient ambience for delivering a failed moment in time.

Well thanks for such a fun and pleasure squasher, for disrupting what could have been a most superb and amazing satisfaction.

Said CK:
What is it? And why are you swearing?

Bo responded:
We, have, to go, like now, and fast! Why? CK inquired.

Bo tried to assure her. Please let's just calmly and quietly, but quickly let's pick up and run.

Well the "Run" word could not have uttered fully when CK turned to her starboard-side as to be on a boat where suddenly danger shows to the right whereas she was facing their snacks as to the bow of the boat with their drinks on the ground.

Well just one glance to then notice this early in the evening the obvious black with bright white stripe from head to tail and she needed no further telling or permission but to dash to the portside for the ***"I'm leaving port" and gone she was!***

Well, Jamaicans naturally have the ability for being fast runners. Well she now proved just how swiftly she could run, and although not born in Jamaica, however her roots are of Jamaican heritage.

Well Boise, being brave and courageous managed to collect her belongings very cautiously then took to the running in the same manner.

Skunks are naturally nocturnal mammals and prefers the dark while to sleep during the daytime, nevertheless; their den being located in the woods and the dark shaded zone were not expecting human company, thus the Mamma skunk was ever nagging to Pappa skunk to go and see, because we have young ones to care about.

CHAPTER – 34-7 Ж꜀

THE ARBORETUM EDUCATIONAL & RECREATIONAL PARK

https://landscapes.northeastern.edu/harmelin
k-arnold-arboretum-franklin-park/

Reference Included in chapters as:
*FOOTNOTES FROM OTHER OBSERVERS **(FFOO)***

These comments help us to track where and whence came CK-Kuya. What school(s) she may have been enrolled in or went.

PORTRAYING A TYPICAL FOLKLORIC CULTURE:

It's the oral history that is passionately upheld and preserved by the Jamaican (Caribbean) people, encompassing traditions unique to their culture. These traditions comprise music, stories, history, legends, and myths. Folklore is lovingly passed down from one generation to the next, kept alive by those who actively participate in and cherish this rich heritage.

As time passes, each new generation evolves based on their passions and experiences, potentially causing the original culture to fade into obsolescence, much like species facing extinction.

To prevent this, individuals or organizations must identify and preserve these invaluable aspects, reviving and refreshing them to captivate the current generation, while also reminding the past generations of the true essence of their cultural heritage.

Jamaica Plain vividly portrays the vibrant blend of Caribbean culture and especially the Jamaican folklore, embodied by the energetic performances and agile movements infused with a distinct sensuality, seemingly exclusive to Jamaicans.

That by an initial glance to the first sight of those moves was like being caught in a relentless magnetic pull, triggering an uncontrollable cascade of muscular contractions. The mesmerizing allure of these spirited dances is undeniable, effortlessly drawing observers into their rhythmic embrace.

Even the traditional *'Limbo dance'* transcends societal constraints, as onlookers become fully immersed in the captivating spectacle.

Once drawn in, it felt as if the body was propelled into a whirlwind of involuntary movements, effortlessly executing twists and turns as if on autopilot.

So, when it comes to doing the *'Triple-L (Limbo) Like me dancing'* no one who did the dance really cared about what their spread open legs or crotch were displaying.

Then, once it came down to CK's turn to do the *'Limbo, Limbo, Limbo like me...'* dance, it seems as though by a spell; she had completely lost her morals and dignity in front of Boise who was by now with ecstasious mental fatigue while looking on with such a strong gaze as though being invited somewhere.

But then; In a poignant moment and to his astonishment, that sort of (*'New-to-him) dance'* had begun to pick him up; to stand up straight to the forehead, like a young mythical Unicorn, heated as it were; with a fiery whipping tail that had stretched all the way to the point, and from whence came those skunks that had interrupted passionate opportunity.

CHAPTER – 34-7a ЖꝄ

SALLY'S COMPASSIONATE WITH CONFESSION:

Now it's Sally who once again had suddenly disrupted his seemingly intimate gaze… But only this time, Sally had continued to be menacing his attention; however, inquiring and asking compassionately, she now confronts Joey about his recurring thoughts of CK, expressing the pain she endures witnessing his wistful daydreams.

She reveals the torment and guilt she grapples with, lamenting the impact of her actions on their lives and her unrelenting inner turmoil.

Boise, though momentarily distant, imparts a message of resilience and acceptance, emphasizing the importance of facing one's actions and memories, as they form the foundation of one's future, then with her badly broken heart now seems to console Boise said:

Sally:

Joey, why are your eyes full of tears and why do you seem so far away not even hearing what I've been saying to you or replying to anything I've said, or asked you?

By this time Boise had slipped out of his daydreaming of being lost in the past with CK and Limbo dancing, have by now responded saying. I'm very sorry CK! I; I meant Sally! I was thinking about CK again. I'm sorry Sal!

Sally retracted:

It's alright Joey, I'm used to this and that by now.

Sally thus confronts Joey, underscoring his recurring thoughts of CK, expressing to Boise for the first time the pain she endures by witnessing his wistful daydreams.

She reveals the torment and guilt she grapples with, lamenting the impact of her actions on their lives and her unrelenting inner turmoil.

Boise, though momentarily distant, imparts a message of resilience and acceptance, emphasizing the importance of facing one's actions and memories, as they form the foundation of one's future.

The emotional intensity and depth of these experiences underscore the powerful influence that cultural traditions and personal relationships hold in shaping our lives, persisting as indelible fragments of our collective narratives.

Sally continued…: But only that; for all the times you've slipped into CK dreamland in front of me; that just terrorized me to my own guilt and I don't know what or how to prevent from crying over the loss of both of you, which brings me nothing but nightmares and traumatic bewilderment and fears of such that you have no idea or about what that's all doing to me.

If only just once; you could get into my secret life to know what torments me over all those years of feeling and dealing with the cruel, bad, nasty and unjust things that I've done to you and have caused to both our lives, our friendship and to CK as well.

I was very selfish and jealous of you and CK. I wanted to have you back or for even a piece of you Joey, and per my plot I got exactly what I wanted, but I had no idea that it would turn out this way.

I am the one at fault for what has happened between you and CK even though we don't know one thing about where she went, is she still alive or dead, what she is or has suffered, yes or no we don't know.

Nobody knows only God alone. My life has been but hell! Burning Hell! Joey! And I wish nobody would ever do what I've done, and I've even given thoughts of turning myself in to the authorities for punishments for my crime, but they have no punishment for this, and I fear the punishment from God at judgment day. I don't even believe that God will ever forgive me because I did this to you and CK.

Whenever I said "Good morning" or good day, or night, whenever I replied to someone who've asked how you are Sally, it's every time a lie when I replied that I'm doing alright or doing well or some BS of such and such, and that all are but stinking dirty and shameful, rotten lies.

Because to see in my heart and mind it's dark and misty and full of lies and torments because of what I've done to you Joey. I feel that God is punishing me for being such a bad person to have destroyed your life and my friend's life.

Boise's response was just the sound of; hmm! Whatever that means? Maybe that meant as to say, when someone has concocted a plot, it should include the what's to follow afterwards, because life does move forward whether we like it or not and what one has or have done does follow us and not left behind.

Those are what our future is based on and as well; it becomes part of one's life cycle building blocks or foundation. One needs to see that much ahead and to determine how to live with those elements that you cannot shake or change which are our memories.

Boise then turned to sally and by a gentle hug consoling her and said:

Boise:

Sally! Sally! Don't worry so much, you are a good person. You've done alright in life. You are getting married now so cheer up and don't worry about me so much. There's no need for that so let's move on. Yes!

Sally is interjecting… But Joey.…...

Joey persisting:

Sally, what's more it's not just you, it's me as well! I'm at fault in every way. Although as drunk as I became does not negate the fact that I'm equally guilty, because I could have declined the first alcoholic drink, I could have not taken the second or third because I was still un-inebriated and quite sober but how and what you did made me to fully felt I was in paradise, and I didn't want to leave it.

Sally:

Rightly so, and that was my cruel concocted plans, because I wanted you so badly and I would've done anything at that time because I was way too jealous.

Boise:

So, you see that, even well ahead of that drink I should have not been with you alone in the first place and because I was already engaged to CK, so friend or not I should have not been there at all. Whether I was drunk or not, I'm still guilty.

Guilty also because the alcohol is most certainly not meant for the body to ingest. So, we are both suffering for what could have or may have caused to happen with CK.

Even so, here we are arguing about whether she is dead or not, when perhaps and hopefully so, that she had found someone, *got married and with her family as we speak.* So, I think we should let her go now.

Sally:

Well Joey, you are right and *since you have touched on the matter of marriage,* I wanted to marry you, and only you Joey, but now that I've a daughter and now getting married to her father so I must proceed with that now. So, will I see you at the wedding? I already have enough disappointments in my life so just please be there, will you Joey?

Well in and throughout all this conversation and catching up of Boise and Sally, that the ghost of CK had been there all along.

In fact, due to the spiritual connection of Boise and Charlie-Alice meant that they are both soulmates to each other, and so when together in spirit their full connection becomes one for all eternities.

Thus, CK can never leave Boise, but to be with him through his life as more than a Guardian Angel (GA) to him.

CHAPTER – 34-8 ӜꙄ

THE MAN ADAM AFTER HUMAN LIFE

Adam & Hawwa/Eve (H/E) they belong without exception or substitution, without any exchangement or replacement.

As it's been written pertaining the man Adam, that when he was created, in that body possessed both male and female in one, thus they belonged with each other before mortal life, in and through mortal life, and as well after mortal life.

Note that ('it is a belief'), that the human Body (person or people) were created beginning with Adam & Hawwa/Eve for the purpose of hosting the spirits; God had placed in them, which are truly what we are (Spirits).

IE: We are Spirits! Not humans! Human is the name of the physical house (Body) where we (Spirits) live or is hosted for a period of time.

Note an observation to be considered: We are all here to learn in this great University called Earth.

[No house was purposely or specifically designed, developed, made or meant for just one person alone to occupy for and throughout his or her life].

Consider the body then as being the 'House'!... How many spirits live there? How many visits there for multiple reasons? For reasons such as for permanent residence, temporary residence, visiting for all the reasons and even that of a doctor's house call, a plumber's repair service call, a relative dropping in to check on the resident and other reasons,

In the first place the man (Adam/human) was created from the earth and given eyes to see the physical world, objects and all physical elements, but not with the physical eyes to specifically see any spiritual entities.

Nor (*as we know it*) can the eyes be evolved to accurately see to then be able to identify spirits.

No human eyes or knowledge can specify or make any accurate reference, comparison with any other spiritual forms or state.

Nor can any human form be compared to what God form or image is (*i.e., if God has one as we do not know that as being factual).*

No human being has seen God. 'We only learned that God is what a Spirit is, and spirits are not visible to any human eyes.'

No one can say or comment on what any spirit looks like.

God does not have any form that any human can conceive, comprehend, make references to describe, compare or assume any resemblance to what God is. Yet it is a belief that; the human form and being was created with the characteristics and the (spiritual) likeness and all of those spiritual definitions of which God is said to be.

Thus, any comments regarding God's image written in any books or verbal comments, are all but speculations and nonacetate in any language, religion or cultural sect of people or per the generations past or current.

Thus, we are reminded henceforth; to see past and beyond everyone's (human being) various and different interpretations. It is always our interpretations that get us all in trouble for disputing who is right, who are not and to the most part the humans are all dead wrong about what God is or created us to do and be.

That is because there are too many personal speculations that add and take away from the original that confuses the entire concept of what God is or about.

(Bible-kjv) Psalm 82:6 *(I have said, <u>Ye are gods</u>; and all of you are children of... {instead of creations of} ...)*

(Bible-kjv) John 10:34 *("Is it not written in your Law, 'I have said <u>you are "gods"</u>?)*

Adam from then possesses all the characteristics and qualities of his creator that for whatever Adam possesses; it therefore confirms that all humans possess the very same.

Thus, what God wants us to know, during creation God has placed all the basis of that knowledge already with the spirits' memory and humans by their individual spirits can access that information similar as any animal or bird can navigate what, where and when they desire.

Humans possess the similar whereas those are acknowledged due of what is inherent or spiritual and only happens when one can acknowledge things from the spiritual perspectives and not from the physical.

Thus our spiritual abilities became inefficient and corrupted, due to the sins of: Lust, greed, excessive pridefulness of the various physical wants and desires that voids our spiritual abilities.

That also due to the various wars, due to the likeness of acquisitional lust, confrontations and all the likes of what sin is due to.

The man bearing in himself; also being both male and female, being created perfect in every way, until the female was drawn out from him, whom he named as *Hawwa or Eve (H/E)*. This rendered him imperfect and unlike prior female removal.

So then, take a look further and beyond all that the eyes can see, that there can only be one specific female to each male. Even so the difference in age could be as much 75 to 80 years apart for reasons with that as in a rebirth occurrence if one had died early and rebirth at a time when one of the mates remain alive to old age.

For if one remains worthy of a rebirth can happen sooner than later. A rebirth needs to happen if one host had died and never found its true mate had to rebirth for it cannot progress alone.

How many lifetimes does it require? Remember the eternities have no limits and the spirits cannot die. Each rebirth will seem as the first, because the body cannot comprehend or recall what that spirit had experienced, or that it had lived prior or not.

See that no spirit that once occupied a human body can progress into heaven or become an angel unless it is rejoined with its spirit half. It is said that through multiple lifetimes, the purpose is to become perfect like God in heaven.

For, hence the statement to reference stating as: "Be ye (you) perfect even as your father in heaven is perfect."

Thus, we see the confirmation and reference to that statement also stating as:

"Truly, truly, I say unto you, except a man (woman) be born of water and of the Spirit, (i.e.; the water-base sperm followed by the entry of the Spirit by some 5-8 weeks (less or more), after the fetus has been formed), cannot enter into the kingdom of God. "Ye (you) 'MUST' be born again!"

We must come up to that stature where and when God can thus say to that one. "Welcome in my good and faithful servant" and "Let Us Create something together." That spirit then would have already regained its male/female self together. Hence no one can go to where God is, unless that one had prior arrived at that successful accomplishment without their missing parts.

SPIRITUAL SEPARATION:

According to the Lord's will, the union of the male and female in the one body resulted in a spiritual separation followed by marriage.

Marriage serves to maintain their connection and as well serves various creative purposes as per God's divine plan for His creations.

The primary purpose of their union, which naturally and uniquely occurs between the male and female, is for procreation, a fundamental aspect across all species on Earth.

God allowed other species to reproduce through parthenogenesis, without the need to separate the female from the male, serving purposes other than pleasure or sin.

Marriage was instituted from that very beginning and has been widely believed in and practiced by generations, indicating its significance and enduring relevance.

ADAM AFTER HUMAN:

All the sentient creations were created for hosting God's created spirits for their specific progression on the Earth and worlds without end and for the purpose of progressing beyond all that is known to human wisdom.

The earth or world I feel is to be considered as the greatest of the Universities that we can ever consider where all humans and the various other creations and species are placed for our learning and for spiritual progress.

Marriage for one; as it seems, can only take place while in life on the earth and while in the human mortal form in terms of people.

When it was time authorized by the Lord God:

The human body is designed for a wide range of physical tasks, achievable only through consistent and rigorous training. This includes the specific purpose of male and female individuals being matched to one another, rather than universally paired for eternity.

According to this perspective, God unites them in life, to live as one in all aspects until they shed their human form. Even then, their spirits continue to remain connected, with no other spirit able to take the place of a specific partner.

This unique connection cannot be replicated, even among many other potential partners. For instance, Adam's connection to Hawa (Eve) would not be the same with any of the ten or more other women he could have married.

Similarly, after Adam and Hawa, every human being must seek out and marry their spiritually matched mate. Just the same as other creatures know how to seek their homes by their inherent instinct to find their offspring and sustenance.

Whereas humans are also endowed with the ability to seek their spiritual matched partner, reflecting the belief that humans were created to be the closest beings to God and knows these things better as they should.

PROFOUND BOND BETWEEN BOISE AND CHARLIE-ALICE (CK).

The connection between Boise and CK is undeniably remarkable. From the very first moment they laid eyes on each other, it was evident that their bond was unique. Their ability to find each other defied all logic, almost as if they were destined to be together.

CK made the courageous decision to leave her previous home and life behind to join Boise although not by any planned or specific connection or person that she had already met and acquainted with, and their meeting marked the beginning of an unbreakable union. Their love knows no boundaries.

- They are willing to sacrifice their lives for one another.
- They endure hardships and suffering in solidarity.
- Even in the face of adversity, they refuse to be separated.
- Their attraction is incredibly powerful, drawing them together against all odds.
- Their connection transcends the boundaries of life and death.

It is evident that their bond is not confined to the physical realm - even in spirit form, they remain inseparable. The depth of CK's yearning for their reunion underscores the intensity of their connection.

Boise and CK's union are more than just a partnership; it is a merging of two complementary spirits, each an essential counterpart to the other. In their unwavering commitment, they embody the profound harmony of opposites coming together in perfect unity.

INNUMERABLE LIFETIMES NEEDED:

In each timeline, individuals will face trials and temptations that they must overcome to prove themselves worthy of rebirth. Therefore, finding one's soulmate in the earliest timelines is incredibly crucial. The guidance emphasizes the importance of living above sin and preparing oneself to be worthy. This involves the requirement of maintaining worthiness to find one's perfect soulmate, a pivotal step before advancing towards perfection and heavenly progression.

BE YOU PERFECT EVEN AS GOD IS PERFECT:

According to the Bible (Matthew 5:48 KJV), only a perfect spirit can exist or dwell in heaven.

Humans can potentially progress to become heavenly angelic beings, such as the Archangels Michael and Gabriel, by reconnecting with their missing or separated spiritual gender.

After human life, spirits in their pure form can serve as guardians, fulfill spiritual duties, or even be sent back to earth as Prophets. To progress, reborn Prophets must find and marry their specific spiritual mate without external guidance.

The criteria for identifying a spiritual match include the ability to resolve issues, maintain unity, and compromise. It does not depend on visual or auditory cues, education, or material possessions. However, humans often lose track of these indicators due to worldly desires and preferences.

Progression is hindered by indulging in vile plots or self-harm, and being guilty for the harm of others. Marriage age is inconsequential as long as it complies with governmental regulations. However, humans lack perfect knowledge of their soulmate.

The key to heavenly progression lies in unity, cohesion, and the ability to work through differences. Signs will manifest if a couple is not meant to be together, indicating that they are not soulmates. Even if raised together, intimate contact cannot compensate for a lack of spiritual connection.

Some Prophets may marry multiple times, while others may remain unmarried if they have already progressed with their soulmate. For example, Adam progressed to become the Archangel Michael because he married his soulmate, Eve.

Procreation is not the primary purpose of human life; rather, it is the spiritual evolution and progression of each created spirit to ultimately transcend the likeness of God.

SO, WHAT EXACTLY IS GOD WE BELIEVE:

God, the creator, is a spirit characterized by love, compassion, forgiveness, gentleness, mercy, kindness, and grace.

God is omnipotent, possessing all power, omniscient with all-encompassing knowledge, and omnipresent, existing everywhere and seeing all.

God gives and takes away life according to divine will, which cannot be equated with murder. God has the authority to create and take back life as deemed appropriate.

While humans may possess the abilities of creation, destruction, and termination of life, these powers are limited to those they bring into existence, except for instances such as warfare or self-defence, where harm to others is not intended or planned.

In all aspects, whether spiritual or physical, God can do all things. Thus, the spirits in the human hosts are here to learn especially how to affect and manipulate any physical mass, whereas God can just speak, consider or select a desire and it's done.

WHAT ARE ALL SPIRITS MEANT FOR:

All spirits were created for heavenly progressions.

All spirits were created with the likenesses of what God is; however, it requires development.

For all the developments required per spirit is for us to become more than that of the likenesses of what God is.

Therefore, we see that for those various developments required; they can never happen in just one lifetime, but it is required to be physically "born again" to experience many lifetimes and live to learn and develop to a perfect knowledge, those attributes.

Thus, you'll have gained the perfect knowledge by the experience of becoming what God is and beyond just the likenesses of God.

That being the case; If a person lived a life and did worked in the health care or medical field will probably not touched any of other physical trades such as to be any of the following such as: Plumbing, Electrical, Hydraulics, Carpentry, Flooring and Masonry, Automechanic, Radio & TV broadcaster or DJ. You can name so many other trades and ask the question: Does God know how to affect or do any or all those things? Yes God does!

Well, that being the case, well you'd better get moving, because your life on earth is moving kind of fast and you need to get caught up, if not you'd be required to have a rebirth, because, if we are to become like God, before we can go to where God is.

Note this; that it is only a qualified spirit that has gained the validations of what a god is, before one can be in the present of God.

It has been stated: [Matthew 5:48 ("You shall therefore be **perfect**, as your Father, who is in Heaven, is **perfect**.")],

[Bible-verse; "You will do greater works than you see me do."

Hence the statement: *[(John 14:12-18 KJV) "Truly, truly, I say unto you, …, the works that I do …, greater works than these shall he do…."]*

WHAT IS MEANT TO BE BORN AGAIN:
NOTE CAREFULLY:

To be <u>born again</u> requires: The liquid <u>water-base sperm cell</u> that caused pregnancy!

Then it requires the spirit that is being hosted!

The speaker had spoken specifically of the actual and natural way for what "Born Again" truly means. Nothing else!

For each phrase, statement or comment that the speaker talked about, was of the actual and specific to mortal or human life that was meant and needed no interpretations other than the specifics.

Otherwise, that same speaker had also noted in another context; Saying: ("…If it were not so, I would have told you…")

CHAPTER – 34-9 Ӝꗭ

UNUSUAL PHENOMENON WITH SPIRITS NOT FAR OFF:

<u>from-CH-34-7a</u>

Boise, having consoled, then turned to Sally and said,

You know, Sally, ever since CK went away, each day I feel as if by some chance I'm feeling her, that she is not far from me. It seems like she is either in the room or in the town, not far from me.

So, as that being the case, I'm always being pulled to where she is and cannot find her.

At times, I feel that I'm hearing her calling me and I'll go to see, but she's not there.

I'll be sleeping and perhaps I have an appointment or something important and I'm running late, but by a pinch on my leg or arm, or a tug at my ear, or the wind passing by my ear, or a pinch on my toe that wakes me up then I'll remember I am to go quickly.

And then, strangely enough, other times in my dreams, I'll hear someone call out my name up to three times till I wake up, and nobody is there. There are multiple other ways and times that I cannot count and if I start writing all the occurrences I've experienced, I'll be writing a book on just my various intuitions of each day.

JOYFUL WATERMELON ADVENTURE

Once, I witnessed a peculiar sight: A watermelon resting on a table after three days in the same position had suddenly started to sway back and forth quite vigorously at 2:30 in the early morning, as if it had a mind of its own.

Fearing that it could roll and fall to the floor and break open then caused me to rush over to prevent it from tumbling to the floor, but when thought about that occurrence had left me quite puzzled as to what could have cause the melon to suddenly be tumbling on its own, so I tried to recreate its unexpected dance, I couldn't.

ELECTRIFYING MOMENT

At another time, it was also 2:30 but in the afternoon this time, and after feeling sleepy from all my activities from the morning, I decided to take a nap somewhere. While peacefully resting, I was abruptly awakened by an unusual commotion. Perplexed by the audacity of someone's relentless attempt to disturb my slumber had caused me to jump up quickly and so confused, because no one was there, but still I hurried to the window.

As I approached the window, to my surprise, I witnessed a sudden burst of light and a bang outside, illuminating the scene. It felt as if the universe had prompted me to capture the moment, including the explosion and the illumination from the electric wires overhead.

Throughout many instances and numerous stories, I have been uplifted by the feelings that led me to believe in a reassuring presence by my side, even though it remained unseen.

A musician named James once mentioned possibly seeing CK the evening before, sparking a strong desire in me to search for her. Yet, the next morning, I strongly sensed her presence. I was convinced she was nearby, but despite feeling her presence everywhere I went, my search proved fruitless.

CHAPTER – 34-9a Ӂℭ

TRIANGULAR-REMORSED:

With the tears in his eyes Boise then said:

Even now as we are here chatting for all this time it's as though she is here for all this time, and I just want to see her so much. So, so much Sally! I want to see her to tell her I'm so sorry!

Sally then broke into tears and they both embraced each other in simultaneous weeping and crying in solemn praying over CK, this for the first time that Sally and Boise begin to share each other's pains and sorrow and grief that CK had suffered, that the triangle had now come together when Sally then exclaimed openly saying calling on God three times.

"Oh God! Oh God! Oh God! Please! I didn't mean for all this to happen to CK. <u>Please forgive me</u> for my sins and the pains I've caused Joey and help us to move forward. We have suffered for many years, and we did not mean any harm to CK.

I was very selfish, and I just wanted to have the man I love in my life for all my years since I was a child. Was that so wrong? If it was, I did not know it. <u>I'm sorry</u> for what I did to Joey that made him come to me because I loved him so very much.

<u>Please forgive us</u> Oh God and let us live in peace for the time we have left in life. And only <u>if I could, but trade my life for CK</u>, my best friend, then <u>I would gladly do it</u> right now.

God, you know my heart that all that I did was out of true love for Joey so much that I did not marry any other for all these years till now. I pray <u>please trade my place right now with CK</u> and <u>I'm willing to go anytime night or day for my life</u> and what's left of it, so that Joey can find his loved one I pray…"

Sally continues to weep with tears that seem to form a river where there was no riverbed and <u>for three times have asked and volunteered her life for CK</u>.

Then something very strange just happened at that very moment. It was although the room went from summer to winter and back to summer again and the silence followed filled the room.

[Reference CH-34-9a]

Follow this section continued in GTNE BOOK-2, Volume-1a, The full novel edition

CHAPTER – 46 ӜϽ

PROVIDE SUPPORT & CARE

The following are true stories found online where CK has been busy working hard in rescuing the perishing and caring for the dying.

There are many, so many times when it was necessary for her to attach herself to those who were still alive, to assist them with the power required to be saved and remain alive. If that meant walking to a safe location, swimming or climbing in some fashion to safety.

Otherwise by any means required for them to get to safety. And yet all the effort for saving lives remains as a dream and people just realized they were saved, but cannot tell who, how or why.

Today's YouTube or Google can verify the many globally occurrences whereas this anonymity as to how those individuals were saved was necessary. Otherwise, to make publications for giving the credits and praises to unseen angels, spirits or ghosts, most people would and will have a difficult time believing or understanding.

I feel that; having made this information public, that it will be easier on us as a people if we are aware of the spiritual things that are happening around us and about us.

This way life will not be so difficult to live and let live as numerous people from all walks of life are having a very difficult time trying to justify whether scriptures are true, or does God exist and if so…, follows with much more questions no one can give any answers bearing from any perfect knowledge.

SONG: [Give Me A Reason, by; Pink]

Only just a few years ago we were slaughtering many more animals for food, for clothes, for sports, for hate and for other unnecessary reasons, but today in many countries the animals are protected to some degree, which is still insufficient, and there are laws governing how animals are being treated.

We still have a very long way to go until we are mostly aware that the lower forms of life all have a right to live their lives as well as we do.

Who knows for certain with any perfect knowledge, that at once upon a time that each of us were not possibly one of those lower forms of life that we now step on and squashed under our feet?

Just think of how dogs are working with us. Think of the horses and that they are progressing as we all do.

Some dogs and horses etc, are working as police personnels while others are still in the wild and, or just roaming the streets or woods trying to find any kind of grubs that they can eat to hold them over until the next few hours. We are not so different.

GOOD SPIRITS

SONG: Hallelujah, by Leonard Cohen]

With regards to the good spirits, there are times when it is necessary that a spirit may attach themselves to a person, especially to carry out their duties in doing good works.

CK has progressed thereby received permission and her orders, so many times this is what she does to rescue the perishing and care for the dying, especially in places such as in India, where at times, there were great numbers of train crashes to the sum of 2000 per year, resulting in too many thousands of people who have died or could have had an untimely death.

Many people have suffered during the Train-wreckage. Many have been rescued by CK and others, especially those who received the special assignment in their human life to perform for the benefit of others, and the world in general.

It is a very common thing for angels to communicate with humans, giving us (humans) assignments for the sake of, and benefit of the many.

There have also been those who had received this said encounter; in such a way; that afterwards, they are said to be a Prophet, or messengers of God.

Others who had received other callings, which required no writing to anyone and so did not divulge that information. Some were restricted to write while with others that was optional.

However, one must bear in mind that, if an angel came and gave any information that was meant to be optional, that does also mean that; that information must have been really and extremely important, or that the source of that information is watching and waiting to see what one would do with that information.

<u>For as an example:</u>

1) In the scriptures; Daniel was given literature and was told to not divulge that it was for the latter day. That he was to close the book on that information.

However, Daniel must have figured that although he was told to not divulge. The angel did not say do not write, yet he knew that for an angel to come to him, must have been very important, and so he felt that he must write it; so that the people would have that information at a later time.

2) There was a certain man named Jonah (a Prophet), who was called and sent to warn a certain people of their wickedness, but it seems that this man would have preferred these people to be dead.

Jonah went and hid himself in various places so as not to deliver the message until he was found on a certain ship, and to the point when he was swallowed by a whale.

He was then vomited by the whale who must have had indigestion from the bad odor of Jonah, who might have not had a shower in months.

Realizing that he could not hide from God, he delivered the message, and the people changed their minds.

3) It is also written that, a certain merchant once assembled a few of his subjects (3 or 4), prior to leaving on his mission. He then had given them each; various portions of investable sums.

Upon his return, he then called together those who had received his valuables, inquired as to their methods of works and diligence, regarding his funds.

But only for one, who was afraid of losing, or put to waste of those funds, as well as had no intention of gaining any further values unto his master. Thus, that one, basically, or otherwise simply hid the funds and upon master's return, had given the exact portion back to his master, whereas with the others, they had doubled, tripled and had given all to the master.

4) Then again, Adam and Eve had received instructions and were left alone to prove their obedience. So, while the gate was purposefully left open so that the thief and liar could enter to put them to the test of obedience. Thus, they failed.

Although failed, they did, yet there was a way provided for further training and repentance, which then led to forgiveness and further progression, except that "thou shall not kill!" Wherein was a lesson learned.

5) I was given this information but thus I was (at first) afraid to write it, unsure of making it public. I felt the promptings; that millions of people are dying each year by homicide and by suicides, also; due to lack of this knowledge.

So, to make this information public, may have saved a few lives, or a few thousands of lives. How could I not write and publish this information? There are many examples that have been recorded, documented and are available publicly, accessible online, which are too many to be mentioned here.

Every person has and knows what 'truth' is. One only needs to be sensitive or to be in tuned with those feelings we feel from time to time, from the GAs who pay visits to every person constantly.

CHAPTER – 47 ӜꙄ

SPIRIT SUBJECTIONS

There are no known human factors that Spirits are subjective towards.

There are no known limits by human standard that can restrict, or slow down any spirits' movements, unless they choose to slow down by attaching themselves to a live human person.

They operate as it were, in a vacuum and are not limited to measurements, distance or time.

Thus, in a fraction of a second, a spirit could accomplish many given tasks, which may involve a human person, before moving on to several other persons, communicating with those persons, and then once the communication has stopped, it would be felt as a dream to that or those persons.

Our natural senses do not have the capacity to measure, or operate above a given number, or level greater than a stated measure of hypersonic speed, or capable of measuring the movements of spirits.

FYI: Consider the meanings of: 'Supersonic means faster than the speed of sound, while hypersonic means specifically five times faster than the speed of sound'.

SAVED IN THE NICK OF TIME

As found online: In India, a train was approaching a certain location on the tracks where a rail had been damaged. If the train had continued at the same speed, it would have completely severed at that broken track, leading to a potential derailment and putting many lives at risk, whereas many had previously suffered from train derailment crashes.

SPIRIT ATTACHMENTS:
<u>SONG</u>: [My Love is Your Love, by; Whitney Houston]

It is believed that CK had selected a 12-year-old boy, and had attached with him, or had prepared him, which is more of an attachment rather than preparation.

Once the spirit has attached to a person willingly or not, the spirit is then able to move that human body (possibly) at the same speed or movement that the person is able or much faster by the spirit's will.

While the human person has human limitations, that is what the spirit or CK has to work with and probably is able to mobilize that person in a way that can generate it's movements at unknown higher speed as well.

ASSUMED EXAMPLE INVOLVING THE GA *(guardian angel)*
(As found online)

Not by any accident, but for a specific reason and purpose, that a twelve-year-old boy from Mangalpur in Bihar, IN, by his bravery and his red T-Shirt saved hundreds on a passenger train travelling to its destination, when the boy noticed a broken rail track.

With the help of the GA and on a day while the temperature was cold to ten degrees, but the boy withstood the cold, and so was able to stand on the track in the path of the speeding oncoming train while waving his red shirt, until the train slowed down and came to a stop.

In all cases that a person had gone out of their normal and had done something of bravery, was due to an inspiration by spirits inside that person, or by other guardian angel.

It is by a desire to be of service to others that does inspire opportunities for good works, as also is the invitation method for invoking our GAs.

CHAPTER – 48 ӜꙄ

QUEEN OF THE SEA-SRI LANKA:

The Queen of The Sea train crash in Sri Lanka, caused by the Indian Ocean Tsunami which struck in December 2004 is regarded as the worst train disaster in railroad history after it caused the death of over 1700 people.

The overloaded passenger train, Queen of the Sea Line, was flooded on the south-western coastal railway line of Sri Lanka, at Peraliya near Telwatta. The train was drowned and destroyed by two waves causing the death of passengers who were packed in eight carriages.

The train was approaching its destination on the way from Colombo to the southern city of Galle, at the time of the tragedy.

NOTE: With this many deaths at the same time, a much larger portal for conveying the spirits (from the mortal or physical side after human life) becomes open. This is the same as saying that the spirits went towards and into the light, as they went to the spiritual side.

It is certainly possible for humans to accidentally wander through the same portal, potentially leading them to different dimensions existing on Earth or elsewhere. While no one knows this for sure, the whispers of thoughts come to me as a possibility. Although it may seem irrelevant at this point in the story, it could prove to be important as the series of books continues, as suggested by CK.

Thus, CK and other spirits saw an opportunity and they did jump through to our physical side of life and remain for some while until they are snapped back to where they came from.

I.E. If they did not attach themselves by permission with some humans, thus they must be sent back to their "<u>Ghost-Train</u>" that has "<u>No Exits</u>" and leaving her with no gained memory of where she had been, where she may ride forever, and be the one that never returns!

Well, did she ever return? No, she never returned, and her fate is still unlearned.

However, during her transfer after the Kendal train crashed; and many more such train wreckages, she arrived in the nick of time during the tsunami, and in time to assist many of the people and children who would have been swept away and died by drowning for sure.

Many of the comments you may read online are true.

SAID THE GIRL WHO WAS SAVED:
(I knew we would all die if I didn›t let go)
The girl lost in the tsunami, rescued by the GA, reunites with her family 10 years later in the future... Whereas, to her (the lost girl), it seems like only a few hours have passed!

I believe that God moves in mysterious ways and has assigned guardian angels at times like these, and more lives would have died.

I believe that Charli-K might have been allowed to cross over to do her part in saving lives.

But did she ever return? No, she never returns, and her fate is still unlearned.

CHAPTER – 49 ӜꙄ

A MIGHTY HAND OF GOD HAD SAVED THEM

God has given commandments, or tasks to angels (GAs), for the salvation of humans. That, in times of need, angels and GAs must return to the earth to accomplish various tasks that they were commanded, as well as for saving those who were not commissioned for passing on that to prevent their untimely passing on.

In other words, each human body that is the host for spirits has a termination period, of when we (all spirits) are to be returned to where we were sent from, although some of the bodies have died before that time, which is termed as the "untimely" death.

I believe that CK (the GA named Charli-K) has been doing her part <u>for the salvation of</u> humans, although her situation to us is very sad and troublesome, yet that is her task until God says otherwise. Remembering that we are stars, satellites, beacons, etc., collecting information and doing other tasks for TGOD, not unto ourselves.

Did she ever return? hmmm! Now, we don't know! Maybe not!

THE TASK OF A GA:
(Saving The Lives of Many)

Recall the incident of Bihar derailment, India June 1981

Numerous times CK and other GAs have been summoned to watch over and assist us from untimely death and other reasons.

Many a time a person may be inspired from hours, days, weeks, months or even years in advance, and have been spiritually prepared on how to save the lives of many all at once.

God by self alone does not go down to save everyone. That is the work of our spiritual guardians (GA), or Guardian Angels. So, if you are waiting for "Father himself" to come down and save you, just take what you get, because that's the way it works!

If you were ever in any kind of danger and a normal person comes to assist you, don't say no!

Thinking that you are waiting on God himself to come down and save you. It ain't gonna happen that way!

It is factual that many have been called, anointed, and have been sent on various missions, which also include us; being a normal human person, could also be sent.

One thing is for certain that when sent it meant that that individual was prepared or was entertaining a GA at that moment even as I've experienced multiple times.

I also encourage you to search your various doings to realize that some things had happened with you and you yourself aren't able to decipher to the extent or actuality of what had happened, but you just shook back your shoulders and said, Oh well! Just let it go for nothing.

Well you may be incorrect. You may have been assisting GAs to save lives and not even realized your good works towards others.

Whenever you've gone out of your way to assist others in any way or form, do you suppose that you were doing all by yourself? Well think again and rethink it over.

MIRACULOUSLY CHANGED - EXTENSION OF TIME:

Many have died a different kind of death; where their heart had not stopped, but that they had been miraculously changed (transformed), wherein; their course prolonged as they had been spiritually prepared for a certain spiritual work, which; that one; was meant to accomplish.

I feel I'm one of such wherein for multiple times I may have died, yet I'm still here preparing multiple projects outside my normal or trained skills

I have been inspired to develop this work and I have quit multiple times, because I couldn't physically determine how it would be possible to accomplish such a huge task while at age 67, as well in sectors of business I had not been trained.

Yet I was constantly encouraged to keep writing and preparing for various tasks

Where in, many people throughout our history had experienced this similar change that they themselves had not realized concerning what had happened with them.

Even so, had they realized their personal change, could not speak of such things, as there is, or was, nothing, and no way to prove to anyone concerning this change, any more than ghost can be seen with normal eyes, yet there are those who were prepared and made able to discern such a phenomenon.

And yet, this fact of change has also occurred in all cultures and religions across the world where God is believed to be the creator of the Earth.

So then, at times; it is only after that said death of a person, that one becomes aware of what task they were to go and do, and yet the body itself will still die a normal death at a later time in the future after the tasks were accomplished.

I feel I am one of those people.

[Psalms 82:6-7 King James Version (KJV)
But ye shall die like men and fall like one of the princes].

I was marked with an aggressive type of cancer that also killed my dad within seven months after the diagnosis, yet I'm here after (currently) eight years having never received any pills for medication to this point.

Nonetheless, my journey as others did; must come due in some time after I've accomplished to the extent I was assigned.

BLACK ICE:

I've slid on black ice and had advanced through a red traffic signal stop light and crashed (cheek to cheek) where that is usually by a T-bone crash at 40+ KMPH.

I can also name eight other times prior.

CHAPTER – 58 Ж꒭

WHY CAN'T YOU SEE ME
<u>SONG</u>: [Why Can't You See Me, by; Concrete Blonde]

Think of it, she tries many times to tell a person to put away the gun, or to not jump over the bridge, and other attempts to save someone's life, but because that person don't believe that there are GA(s) at work has dispelled their opportunity for continuing their lives and a chance of completing their earthly progression.

I am sure that, to CK, it would make her very happy just to realize that we knew that she might show up and be able to communicate with us. That thought to her my friends would be like finally going home to family from her prisonlike train.

WHEN YOU BELIEVE
<u>SONG</u>: [When You Believe, by; Whitney Houston and Mariah Carey]

The concerns although, it still remains that she is just a ghost, and although spirits do communicate with people, one must first be gifted or highly sensitized for such a thing to be realized otherwise with clairvoyance abilities. Of that I'm not saying I am!

Even if one is not specifically gifted, rather sensitized that way, it might still be possible for this to happen; after one has trained your level of belief that we, all humankind is but hosts to our spirits and that is what we all are.

Having done so you'd have learned how to respond to your Gut-feelings and promptings when they come to you.

Many times, I would be doing something, at different moments or time, be it day or night, and for some uncertain reason I would suddenly notice various things happening around me.

Things like a white bird's feather or the type from a winter coat, on the floor beside me where I sat, to then have me wondering as to how did that get there?

And also: How did I know at that moment to look down to the floor where that feather was resting on the floor that I never noticed before?

Other times I would find a regular size white feather on the street where I was walking, or a white feather just blown by me through the air by the wind.

Even now, February 2020 I still have a white feather in my car that I found on the back seat of my Uber vehicle.

I didn't see who would have left it there, but it had to have been placed there by one of my riders no doubt. This may not be of any ghostly or spirit meaning of such either, but what do we know?

Other times, I would oversleep, but when it was time for me to be up and getting ready for work, when it felt that someone shook me and I realized that I had to then rush to get to work, or to an appointment.

FOLLOW YOUR GUT ALWAYS
It is all by those promptings that I am able to write this novel.
I am usually very surprised by the results of following these promptings and Gut-feelings that I received, and that by doing so I feel that they might have saved my life a number of times over; already.

From the things I write here throughout this novel, you can make your own assumptions to that regard.

CHAPTER – 58-1 ЖꙨ

OVER THE COURSE OF 60 MORTAL YEARS:

By the various work and experience that was gained to Charlie-K, she had advanced to become a Guardian Angel for only after all spirits have rejoined with their one specific mate can any be advanced to heavenly duties.

CK is thus now able to do a great work and also remembers each and every task completed as shall be mentioned in the CK Kuya Book-2 Volume-1a, the second edition and full novel wherein this is the Introduction to the characters of this Ghost Train No Exits novel.

☆ 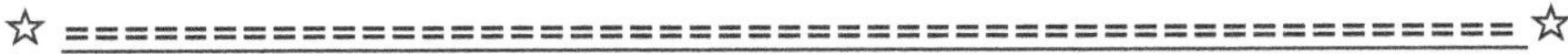 ☆

CHAPTER – 34-4 Жꙻ

THE SOURCE
[Reference CH-34-4 Continuation]

☆ **<u>FYI:</u>** Below is a link to online third-party providers, where readers find additional sources as existing support & information to these CK Kuya stories.

☆ **<u>I.E.:</u>**

- From this ***Ghost Train No Exits*** (GTNE) first edition novel,
- From three other CK Kuya books in a series of four:

  ○ One book planned for publishing per year – 2024, to 2027,
  ○ The initial four books as the leader-novels of multiple books to follow.

☆ OBSERVE:

  ○ A) The first & main character is a ghost that does not age…,
  ○ B) does not fade, but progressively gaining power!

☆ WRITERS CLUB:

Readers & members who love to write, are offered to submit as many chapters relating to the characters & the stories-plot. Everyone then; by progressive default, becomes co-authors and members in this ongoing CK

Kuya series of books, CK Kuya live theatre musicals, along with all the various benefits and incentives mentioned in BAWT-Inc.

☆ CK KUYA SOURCE MONOLOGUE

CK Kuya first leader novels are sequels. Its progressive 5-year mission segments presenting Jamaica-Caribbean *Mento-music as a Throwback* to its *Cultural Art & Entertainments venue.*

- It depicts *Jamaica's folkloric Performing Arts,*
- *It's meant for Global franchising,*
- *For Multinational-inclusions,*
- **And for Multi-cultural disciplines** that are based on the GTNE novels series.

☆ JAMAICA CULTURAL MENTO SONG OF THE PERFORMING ARTS

https://music.apple.com/us/album/jamaican-mento-musi c-hits-1952-1958/504182429

☆ *CULTURAL ART & MENTO THROWBACK*

This development & project was conceptualized in Toronto, Ontario, Canada as presented by; <u>Michael A.</u> *(Blackhall & Associate)* <u>Fareeha Khan</u> (who has inspired this entire business inception. With the exception that, we are sharing with all members. From the Free members to the paid (Elite) members.

We have set the membership fee as extremely low and affordable so that all and literally EVERYONE-CAN!

☆ MEMBERSHIP

Thus, for the purpose of <u>*Paying Forward,*</u> by the *CK Kuya inspiration,* invites all readers to join its membership:

All members become entitled to at least one (if not multiple) "FREE" luxury global vacations **(perpetually)** per year.

☆ MEMBERS BENEFITS:
(Annual vacations - No purchase necessary):

That for wherever members are located globally they can request a complementary luxury vacation gift certificate for vacations to as many as 140 participating destinations globally.

☆ NOT FOR SALE:

These CK Kuya vacations are not for any winnings, not for sale and has nothing to do with any kickback, affiliate marketing or timeshare presentations.

Those are on account of a paid incentive and marketing overhead expense, inspired by; and to CK Kuya development.

☆ MEMBERSHIP FEES

The only membership fee imposed are for the purpose of lowering the BAWT-Inc Limousine service price, that allows or includes all People who are of low-income earners (such as: Seniors on low or fixed budget and students), may afford to call for and to afford Luxury Limousine rides, even on a daily basis.

☆ INVITATION:

- All members are invited to join *(CK Kuya Writers Club)*.
- Write just a couple or few chapters of what you feel, perceive, believe or that you are **(fictionally)** acquainted with CK, Boise or Sally.

☆ BECOME CO-AUTHORS

Members who like to write but never making anything of what they have written. Be that: Poetry, Poems, other stories.

- **HERE:** Members are invited to write mostly any context appropriate to enhance this story series and become co-authors in the CK Kuya compilation for passive earnings as co-authors. NO EXTRA MEMBERSHIP FEES REQUIRED.

- Every member potentially a 2% segment shareholder in the organization of *(Blackhall & Associate World Travel Inc.)*.

No cash investment required. ***Inquire at: <ckkuya.com> or <batravel.ca>. Via WhatsApp 1-416-509-5805.*** *Email to:* *bawt@batravel.ca* *or* *support@ckkuya.com*

==

☆ *CK KUYA* MENTO HONOR THROWBACK

Presenting Jamaica's 'Cultural Art & Entertainments starting in Toronto, Canada as part of reviving its aged and fading cultural folklores:

- *For honoring Jamaican Legends, Cultural Icons, the late folklorists and the Caribbean lyrical balladeers as well as cultural activists,*
- *For acknowledging to preserve their work and legacy,*

*All of which in general truly belong to **Jamaica's Cultural Performing Arts.***

☆ MENTO FORM OF ENTERTAINMENT

This is also just one type or genre from the Jamaica's earlier cultural entertainments that most people (presumably) under the age of 40 have not heard about as now being presented:

- *As part of **CK Kuya's (Jamaica) Cultural Excursion ideas,***
- *As a form of wooing our tourist guests starting from Toronto, Ontario, Canada,*

☆ *CK KUYA MENTO TORONTO*

*The latter is **for presenting the Jamaica Cultural Experience, particularly** while vacationing in Jamaica.*

This very form also meant for presenting in Canada to Canadians, to those with restrictions to travel, thus presenting this mode of inclusions allowing to experience this sector and form of Jamaica's cultural entertainments from right here in Toronto.

'Mento-Throwback' is as a breath of fresh air.

- A fresh idea for entertainments in the Performing Arts and Theater,
- It was also meant for presenting a new wave of **"Paying Forward,"**
- It's meant for assisting everyone to realize few or more truths:

    ○ that life is not all about buying, selling,
    ○ nor is it about taking without giving back.

☆ PER CK KUYA DEVEOPMENT IT IS PERCIEVED THAT LIFE IS LARGELY ABOUT:

Giving without Selling, and many have missed their moments of such giving!

☆ *GHOST TRAIN NO EXITS*

From a teenage love triangle to the slipping off the rails!

☆ THE AUTHOR'S BIO:

MICHAEL A. BLACKHALL

Michael A. Blackhall, a proud son of Jamaica, is a versatile individual making a mark as an author, entrepreneur, and visionary. His novel *Ghost Train No Exits* marks the beginning of an extraordinary series, inviting collaboration from passionate writers. Michael's diverse experiences, coupled with his Caribbean heritage, shape his unique storytelling, promising an exciting literary journey for readers.

Embracing his Jamaican roots, Michael infuses his storytelling with vibrant cultural elements, transporting readers to the captivating landscapes and rich traditions of the Caribbean. His entrepreneurial spirit shines through his writing, as he weaves together tales of resilience, creativity, and the vibrant tapestry of human experience.

Furthermore, his visionary outlook extends beyond the pages of his novels, as he actively seeks to engage with fellow storytellers, encouraging a collaborative and inclusive approach to creating captivating literary works.

Through his dedication and passion, Michael aims to inspire emerging writers to explore their own unique narratives and voices, fostering a vibrant community of literary expression as well as in and through the Performing Arts Triple Treat for the entertainment it brings.

With each new work, Michael invites readers on a thought-provoking and immersive journey, where the echoes of the past intertwine with the possibilities of the future, creating an enriching and unforgettable literary experience so that *"EVERYONE-CAN!"*